A Modern Christmas Carol

A Modern
Christmas Carol

Bob Seidensticker

A MODERN CHRISTMAS CAROL

ISBN 978-1492129011

Cover artwork by Kyle Hepworth

To Sandy, Bobby, and Genny

First Stanza

Reverend Nathan Thorpe strode into the makeup room of Hundredfold Studio, grimacing as he finished the last set of dumbbell curls. He dropped the dumbbell on the carpeted floor behind the middle chair of the three and took his seat.

Above the wide mirror on the wall was the ministry's logo, overflowing baskets of yellow wheat. Or perhaps gold coins—the ambiguity was deliberate.

"Morning, Mary," he said. "Let's get this done so you can go home. Any plans for Christmas Eve?"

Mary shook out a starched white barber cape. "It's just us tonight, but we have family coming for Christmas Day. We'll have a packed house. And you?"

Nathan scanned the schedule for the day's broadcast. "It'll be quiet for us this year." In fact, it was quiet for Nathan most years. He was recently estranged from his wife Janice, his second, after she stumbled across his latest affair. The couple had also been growing apart from conflicting views of the progress of the ministry—the power and acclaim invigorated him, while she was done with the limelight and wanted a quieter, more honest life.

With no children, there was plenty of space in their mansion for them to make their separate lives and keep up appearances. Janice was still professional, and, to her credit, she convincingly played the game during each broadcast as singer and supportive Christian wife. For now, at least.

Mary snipped at his hair as Peter Baldwin appeared in the doorway.

"Nathan, is now a good time to review inventory?" Peter ran the merchandising department. He was quite overweight and enjoyed junk food flamboyantly. He wore the same dark jacket every day, regardless of the season, and dandruff from his medium-length black beard always speckled it, something Nathan couldn't un-notice.

But fashion sense and hygiene weren't in Peter's job description, and most of the ministry's 110-million-dollar annual revenue came in response to giveaways that he thought up and packaged—prayer shawls, vials of River Jordan water, cross necklaces, plaques, statues, anointing oil, and even cell phone bling and rear-view mirror danglers. This was what they mailed out in return for "your most generous seed offering of at least twenty dollars."

Nathan glanced at the wall clock. He'd be on in 43 minutes. "Now's a good time," Nathan said, as he picked up a tennis ball and rhythmically squeezed it. "What have you got?"

Peter turned a page on the papers he held as he walked in. "I've checked with my suppliers and know what I can get in reasonable quantities and with decent prices for January."

Decent prices were sixty cents apiece. Reasonable quantities were 5000 units with a guarantee of quick delivery of at least 30,000 more if demand became high. A giveaway that connected well with the audience would bring in an average donation of 65 dollars plus deliver that all-important home address to which Marketing would mail out additional appeals.

"We had good luck with our Christmas promotion, so I thought we might try frankincense next year," Peter said. "I mention it now because we'll get better prices if we lock in soon."

This year's myrrh had almost been one of Peter's rare failures. The supplier dramatically underbid his competitors, which, in hindsight, should've been a warning. When their Chinese packager received the "myrrh," it wasn't the fragrant yellowish-brown nuggets that the encyclopedia showed but 400 pounds of a sticky red-amber goo. They guessed that it was pine sap.

With no time for a Plan B, Peter had it relabeled as Balm of Gilead, the fabled curative mentioned in the Bible. It smelled like turpentine, but it became their most lucrative Christmas campaign.

"Frankincense sounds good," Nathan said, as he switched his tennis ball to the other hand.

Peter made a note. "Okay, for January, I was thinking sandalwood bookmarks, 71 cents laser etched with the logo, and 89 cents with a tassel. Sandalwood smells nice."

"Is it native to Palestine?"

"No. Ours would come from Australia."

"That's pricey."

"The final work is done in Israel, which gives cachet."

"Where in Israel?"

Peter turned a page. "Haifa."

"No pizazz. Can we truck them through Jerusalem? Bookmarks 'from Jerusalem' might work."

"I'll check." More notes.

"How were online sales this year?" Nathan said.

The ministry's store sold several hundred homegrown items—DVD and CD versions of repackaged sermon series plus over a dozen books ghostwritten for Nathan. It also stocked more than seventy products produced by guests on the show, on which Hundredfold took a fifty-five percent cut of sales. International sales were significant, an area in which they had been an industry pioneer.

Peter turned more pages. "Online sales were up twelve percent."

Mary removed the cape, balled it up, and set it aside. She shook out a new one for the makeup.

In the mirror, Nathan saw his script writer standing in the doorway.

"Peter, are we done?"

"We're done. I'll get you some answers in a few hours." He glanced at Mary. "And there's another issue we need to discuss, but we can do it then. It's rather important."

Peter left, and Malcolm Canon leaned against the sink to replace him. Malcolm was quiet, not much at small talk. He'd had a lucrative career ghostwriting for celebrities, turning rambling narcissistic stories into bestselling gold in months, and he was Nathan's secret weapon. With his growing empire, Nathan had offloaded to Malcolm the scripting of his sermons.

"Good timing. Let's talk about the lineup in two weeks." Nathan had realized since his earliest days on stage that he was in the entertainment business, and crafting a sermon that crackled with energy was demanding work. With Malcolm behind him, Nathan could consistently discourage the audience at one point and show the church as the solution at another, and then finally bring them to their feet before the Ask.

"I want something on tithing," Nathan said. "Let's make it an undercurrent for the next couple of weeks."

"Could be a third rail."

"I don't want to hit it hard. Show me reluctant."

"Maybe you're responding to a letter. Someone wrote in for advice on how donating should be done."

"Good—say that I wouldn't bring it up at all except that someone asked. Give me the letter on paper—that'll make a good prop. And emphasize that tithing doesn't mean *giving*, it means giving *ten percent*."

"Got it."

"And we haven't hit homosexuality lately," Nathan said. "That always connects with the audience."

" 'Thou shalt not be gay' is an easy commandment for most people to follow."

"But here's the trick—we've got a lot of gays in the audience. The donation demographics showed that last time we were too critical. What I want is for straights to feel that this is an easy win where they can feel superior, and for the gays to feel guilt without alienation. We become the solution to that guilt, we harness it. Okay?"

He waited for Malcolm to finish writing. "What have you got to tie this into current events?" Nathan asked.

Malcolm tapped his pencil against his pad of paper. "There was story a few days back about a high school club for gay students. Some parents objected."

"That'll work. Put out a press release in response to the gay club. I'd like that in the queue today. After Christmas, the media will eat up fresh stories."

Mary had finished the makeup and unsnapped the cape. "You look fabulous. Have a great show."

Nathan stood and looked in the mirror. "Thanks, Mary. And Malcolm. Merry Christmas."

He tossed the tennis ball into a corner and picked up the dumbbell, curling it as he walked back to his office.

In the early days of his career, Nathan struggled to package himself in a memorable niche. He needed a way to stand out from his competition. He could've been the guy with the Lincoln beard, or the man sensitive to women's needs, or the one with the jokes, or the emotional one. After trying on a few personas, he decided on the beefcake route. He stood six feet, two inches tall, and that gave him something to work with. He exercised, dieted, tanned, took lots of supplements, and had maintained a lean 220 pounds since his twenties.

Other televangelists often wore polyester to seem in touch with their audience, but Nathan dressed like a model. Now he bought custom suits from Savile Row in London at 4000 pounds apiece, keeping pace with changes in fashion.

He'd had dress shirts tailored to hug his Adonis figure, but now he preferred knit turtlenecks, custom made to cover his torso and arms like paint—basically turtleneck muscle shirts. He would usually discard his jacket halfway through at an emotional high point and turn his stage into a catwalk, pacing up and down and gesturing to support the sermon.

As he turned the corner to his office, that vague comment by Peter popped back to mind and took on an ominous cast. What could he want to talk about?

CȜ

Nathan was still curling his dumbbell as he stopped at the desk of his secretary Sophia Becker. Sophia's fashion sense was far more conservative than necessary, even for a Christian ministry. Some days her goal seemed to be the suffragette look and other days, Christian burqa. She occasionally wore a scarf and Nathan had several times in years past encouraged her to remove it, but she never would. Whatever feminine assets she had, she covered, but that was fine with Nathan. She was competent, and he didn't need any more office temptations.

"Morning, Sophia. What's on today's agenda?"

"You have James Truman from Ethical Christianity at eleven, and then a free afternoon."

Nathan didn't remember who that was but figured that he'd find out when necessary.

Sophia had tended to Nathan's needs for sixteen years at Hundredfold, managing his calendar, running errands, and in general making his life easier. A photo on her desk showed her twelve-year-old daughter Kay hugging Sophia, with both smiling at the camera. Though she had planned more children, Sophia stopped with Kay because she had Down syndrome, heart disease, and other medical issues, and Kay was all she could handle. Sophia discovered the problems in the first trimester of the pregnancy and considered an abortion, but her husband and Nathan had insisted that no one could interfere with God's plan.

Nathan glanced up at the color photos high on the wall. He was CEO and board chair, and his was the larger center photo in a row of the nine members of the Hundredfold board. Like marriages to Solomon, board positions were given to show favor or appreciation, and Nathan wasn't above yanking one as retribution. In return for eating a catered lunch and attending monthly *pro forma* meetings, board members—mostly industry leaders—received 70 to 250 thousand dollars per year. Unlike a typical nonprofit board, the CEO did not answer to them. The photos suggested accountability and transparency to visitors, but Nathan was the perpetual monarch.

He walked into his office, set down the dumbbell, and dropped into the chair behind his big desk. He looked at the desk clock—22 minutes to show time—and returned to the show notes that Malcolm had prepared.

He lifted his head in response to a feminine cough. Sophia stood in the doorway. She usually walked in and completed her business quickly. Hesitation at the doorway wasn't a good sign.

"Nathan, could we talk about some philanthropic ideas?"

He looked at his watch.

"This'll be quick."

He waved her in with two fingers. He'd put her off with some busy work a few weeks earlier, but apparently she wasn't taking the hint.

"I checked on some charities like you asked." She put a sheet in front of him. "These are the most reputable ones that work in East Africa."

Nathan scanned the list. "We can spend money on lots of things, but it needs to have a return."

"This would be good to do."

"Like I said last time, this is a business. 'Good' must mean 'good for business.' We already give money and brag about that. There's just no value in giving a higher fraction." They gave away eight percent of gross revenue, which wasn't bad for their industry. It wasn't like anyone could see their financials.

"But we're a ministry," she said.

"Right—not a soup kitchen. Spending money is an investment, and an investment needs a return—wider satellite footprint, more products in the store, diversified programming to reach a broader audience, that sort of thing. We already have Sudan Christian Relief in this part of the world. We showcased them two months ago."

"They only get twenty percent of what we raise for them, and half of that goes to missionaries."

"Yes, and we have expenses." In truth, fundraisers for their various charities throughout the third world were just one more type of money maker. Nathan considered for a moment challenging her to find something to cut, but she had never seen the ministry's balance sheet or P&L, and even the board saw only a sanitized budget. He wasn't about to give her something to critique.

Sophia said, "I'm just thinking that we might be able to give more."

"Like you said, we're a ministry. If people want to give just humanitarian aid, they can go to CARE or Oxfam."

Nathan thought for a moment about the Rainy Day Fund, the euphemistically named bin that held what in a corporation would be called "profits"—170 million dollars so far, tax free and hidden from judgmental eyes, and growing at a rate of 14 million dollars per year. Only he and the accountant saw these figures. It was all legal, not that they had to worry about an audit.

She hesitated and said, " 'Whatever you have done unto one of the least of these my brethren, you have done unto me' "

Nathan forced a chuckle. " 'I suffer not a woman to teach, nor to usurp authority over the man, but to be in silence.' Now, don't wander into a biblical debate with me, Peanut Head."

Sophia shifted her weight and opened her mouth. Finally, she said quietly, "I was just thinking that we could form a philanthropic foundation. The overhead would be lower."

"Ministries don't create foundations. That just makes no sense." He leaned back in his chair. "Look, I appreciate your concern. Truly. But you're just going to have to trust me with the business decisions."

"Yes, you're right." She took the list of charities. "Thank you for considering it."

Nathan watched her scamper out of the office and gently close the door behind her. Some people just had no business sense.

A few minutes later, Sophia tapped on the door and stepped in. "I have James Truman from Ethical Christianity in the waiting area, here to discuss church transparency. He's your eleven o'clock, but he's early. I can tell him to wait until after the taping."

Nathan didn't remember agreeing to this meeting. In fact, it sounded like a topic he preferred to avoid. He consulted his watch—almost show time. But that would give him an excuse to cut the meeting short. "Let's do it now."

Sophia opened the office door and let in a thirty-something black man, thin with glasses, wearing jeans, sneakers, and a collared shirt. One arm held a tweed jacket and the other a tired leather briefcase.

"Reverend Thorpe," the young man said, "I'm James Truman. I apologize for arriving so early. My flight landed on time and there was no traffic. Thank you for seeing me."

"I'm glad I was able to move things around on the schedule," Nathan said as he gave an assertive handshake. Truman had small hands. Nathan liked to be able to dominate a meeting physically. "I will need to leave soon for a taping. In this business, I answer to the producer, I'm afraid."

"Well, let's get into it, then." Truman set his briefcase across his lap and pulled out some papers. "Ethical Christianity represents a number of reform-minded churches concerned about the lack of transparency in churches and ministries in the U.S. We'd like all nonprofits' financial records open to the public, not just the secular ones."

Nathan guessed that "reform-minded" was code for "liberal." He said, "I suggest a pro-choice approach. Let ministries choose to open their books or not."

Mr. Truman adjusted his glasses. "We think that it's only fair. The taxpayers grant nonprofit status, and in return we show that the money was wisely spent, as promised."

"No one's stopping you. If your churches want to make their records open, that's great. I fully support that choice." Nathan picked up a tennis ball, bounced it a few times on the desk, and squeezed it.

"Our organization represents less than a dozen churches. We'd like to pull in the larger religious community."

"If you'll excuse my saying so, your pitch can't be very compelling if it has attracted so few churches. Tell me—what do you and your 'reform-minded' churches think about separation of church and state?"

"We support it strongly."

Nathan leaned forward onto his desk. "Then let's keep the state out of my church."

"Separation of church and state keeps Mormon prayers out of the public school. It keeps 'God is Great' in Arabic script out of the city hall. It keeps the Hindu god of jurisprudence out of the courtroom. It's the guardian of the believer."

"Eloquent, but I don't remember reading in the Constitution where ministries' private records must be open to the public." The idea of Congress or the public poking around in his finances was to Nathan analogous to someone looking through his dirty-clothes hamper. It was simply no one's business.

"The unfairness is the problem. Why should the nonprofit soup kitchen have to open its books when the nonprofit church across the street doesn't?"

"Why indeed? Are you demanding the right to privacy for all nonprofits? Godspeed."

"Okay, what we're saying is that the religious exemption as it stands now is embarrassing. It says that we have something to hide, that Congress had to help us shield our records from the public, that we'll share the information with God but that we refuse to share it with our fellow citizens. Even those of us with open books are seen as part of the problem."

"And you want Hundredfold to support your initiative."

"We have a public statement urging Congress to require open financial records from all nonprofits. We want the religious exemption dropped. Support from a prominent ministry like yours supporting this would be revolutionary."

"Ain't gonna happen, son—either my support, or your project. We're doing just fine as is." Nathan looked at his watch. "And I'm afraid I need to run." He stood. "Mr. Turner, I appreciate your ideas, truly I do."

"It's Truman." He scooped up his papers. "I caught a 5:15 flight this morning to see you. Am I to only get five minutes? Could we talk after your taping?"

"Schedule's packed, I'm afraid." Nathan stood by the side of his desk and held out an arm toward the door. "I do need to go, I'm very sorry. The producer calls."

Truman seemed to need a moment to regain his bearings and slowly stood. He shoved his papers into his briefcase and walked out. "This isn't over, Reverend Thorpe."

Oh, but I'm certain it is. Nathan watched him leave.

☙

"Hey, Good Looking," he said, minutes later, as he pointed to his color photo on the wall next to Sophia's desk and walked to the studio.

If Hundredfold taped in front of a studio audience, tickets would have been as popular as tickets to the Tonight Show. They had a live audience in the early years, but the people couldn't be relied upon to respond correctly to the ebb and flow of Nathan's sermon.

The result was a sterile and artificial set with a vaguely plastic scent. No one would confuse this with an actual church. The wide stage was brightly lit, and opposite it lay a dark jungle of moveable cameras, thick cables, suspended lights, and technicians.

"Two minutes, everyone." It was the producer's voice over the sound system.

Nathan looked out from behind black curtains on stage right. In front, operators readied their cameras in response to last-minute instructions. A few of the singers and band members adjusted their microphones, the last of the stage hands walked briskly off stage, and Nathan's wife Janice stood ready on the opposite side of the stage.

The cotton candy hair and overdone eye makeup were the extravagance of an earlier generation, and Janice dressed more like a TV morning show host. Today she wore a purple V-neck dress with a cross necklace. Her long blonde hair was parted on one side and pulled back.

They had moved past Janice's rage at Nathan's infidelity, which he admitted was justified, and their relationship had settled into that of two work colleagues who didn't much like each other.

The theme music began over the sound system, the fifteen-second warning. With the conclusion of the first stanza, Nathan put on his smile and walked into the bright lights and canned applause as Janice did the same from the other side. In the center, they clasped hands in their trademarked way and turned toward the audience.

"Merry Christmas!" Nathan said. "Janice and I are so happy you could share some time with us today. We're joined today by the author of a fascinating critique of Darwinism that I know will arm you to fight against this pernicious and mischievous belief."

"I've heard so much about this book," Janice said, "but let's first get into a worshipful mood with a song of praise."

The red light on the center camera winked off and another on the camera facing the singers came on. The singers, two men and two women, began a cappella as Janice made her way to her microphone in the center. The four-piece band kicked in.

A music consultant crafted songs for Nathan that were Christian themed and emotionally powerful. In Nathan's parlance, they were "sticky" and made the audience come back for more. The musicians changed as needed—sometimes acoustic guitar, tambourine, and drums, and sometimes two violins and a cello. Surveys showed that the broader musical range helped broaden the customer base. He had learned early that his production was a thirty-minute infomercial.

With the camera off him, Nathan took his chair center stage. To his left was another for Janice, and on his right, a couch for guests. He reached down for the water bottle behind his chair and took a sip.

Nathan watched the two-song set on the monitor at the foot of the stage. The donation phone number and web site were prominent underneath the logo and the words "Prayer Requests."

The camera returned to Nathan and he stood and led the canned applause for the Hundredfold singers as Janice walked to her chair. They bought their applause as recordings from other televised services.

A large red digital timer beneath the center camera counted down two minutes and forty seconds as they chatted about the social problem of Darwinism and the huge buzz surrounding this new book.

The timer reached a flashing 0:00 as Nathan said, "Let's hear more from the author of the new book, *Evolution: The Adversary Attacks.*"

More canned applause welcomed a small man onstage from Nathan's right. Nathan knew from his bio that he was thirty-two, but he looked like a high school senior at his first prom, eager but intimidated. His suit was baggy, and Nathan imagined his mother helping him get his tie just so.

In fact, the book had earned little attention, but the show was due for another evolution-bashing guest, and the publisher had given them a nice deal.

Nathan shook the man's hand, introduced him to the audience, and waved him toward the couch. As Nathan sat, he said, "Let's see the cover of that book."

The floor director cut to a still of the cover, which showed a drawing of an open-mouthed Tyrannosaur.

"Now tell us about that subtitle, 'The Adversary Attacks.' That's a home run right there."

The small man said, "I see the hand of Satan behind the teaching of Darwinism in science classrooms. Can you believe it? Our own taxes go to pay for atheist propaganda in public schools."

"You can't read the Bible honestly and not see the problem," Nathan said. "We have a choice between the Bible's truth and atheism."

The author paused a moment longer than he should have, and Janice filled the gap. "I really can't see the logic behind theistic evolution, which seems so common among Christians. God hides behind Darwinism? That just seems like accommodation."

"I completely agree." Nathan glanced at his talking points on the teleprompter and back to the author. "Tell us about some of the problems you see with Darwinism."

"Children are pushed from the gospel by our own schools. Surveys show that one of the top reasons young people give for turning from Christianity is that the church rejects science, that the church is out of touch. They point to Galileo, they say —"

"Which is nonsense." This guy wasn't painting the church in the best light, and Nathan's strong voice took control. "Not only does Christianity provide the grounding for the laws of science, but it taught science that nature was regular and understandable. When science and scripture clash, you gonna trust man or God?"

Nathan glanced back at the teleprompter. "Tell us, how do you respond to someone who argues that Darwinism is the scientific consensus?"

"I say that science can be wrong." The author went off talking about Piltdown man and other mistakes in biology.

"Those are great points," Nathan said. "I would add that I trust myself to evaluate the facts. I don't need to rely on scientists when God-given common sense will serve."

"I know how I'd respond," Janice said. "In a contest between science and scripture, it's no contest."

Nathan asked a final question to clarify the book's scope and then encouraged every viewer to get a copy for themselves. He listed additional people who needed copies as belated Christmas presents—teachers, adult children, neighbors, legislators. He was eager to fulfill all these requests, he said, for a love offering of forty-five dollars per book.

He thanked the author and reached over to shake his hand. The small man then smiled in response to the applause and just sat there, looking out into the darkness beyond the cameras as if searching for the hidden audience. Nathan saw a tight shot of himself on the monitor and looked into the camera as he repeated his appeal. In his peripheral vision, he saw the production assistant dash out to shoo the author off stage.

He and Janice took just over six minutes to survey the other work of Hundredfold Ministry—three upcoming live appearances, their outreach in Bangladesh ("which needs your prayers and love offerings"), books by recent guests ("a terrific way to tap these blessings if you missed a broadcast"), and bestselling products from Nathan himself.

As Janice led the singers in another song, a stage hand brought out Nathan's lectern. It was made of clear Lucite with a wireless teleprompter on top. He did six shows a week, and his sermons came out better if he read a carefully crafted text than if he extemporized from notes.

Nathan stood behind the lectern and, prompted by the camera's red light, said, "Friends, Christmas is a time of joy at Hundredfold Ministry, but I must confess that it is bittersweet. This is the anniversary of the passing of a great man, Reverend Lloyd Humbert, the founder of this ministry and my personal mentor and dear friend."

Nathan owed Lloyd a lot, both for his long apprenticeship and for leaving him this media empire on his death seven years earlier. Nathan had been a little naive in the early days. As he came to understand the cash flow, he balked at how little money flowed out to do good works. Lloyd's motto had been, "We scratch their itch, so why not take a little something for our trouble?" Nathan had quickly embraced the logic and enjoyed the lifestyle along with everyone else.

Nathan looked down for a moment—a scripted gesture— and then said, "The thing that Pastor Lloyd taught me, and which I'd like to commend to you today, is to never back down. When you know the rightness of your position, when the Holy Spirit has made clear the meaning of a scripture, you stick to it like a pit bull.

"In this Christmas season we've heard our share of 'Happy Holidays.' And in a Christian nation, founded on Christian principles, people afraid to publicly acknowledge the birth of our savior sickens me. Good Christians, beaten down by political correctness, afraid to fulfill the Great Commission during the season when Jesus fills everyone's heart. In a democracy! You remember democracies, where the majority rules? Well, we're the majority!"

Nathan took off his jacket during the applause and tossed it off camera.

"Pastor Lloyd wouldn't back down. While a young pup, I learned from him how it was done. He showed me what a man filled with the Holy Spirit could accomplish. He'd happily tell anyone he met about America's debt to the Bible. Our Constitution and the Bill of Rights, the fight against tyranny, democracy itself—it's all in the Bible and defended by Almighty God.

"Back then, of course, the atheists and secularists knew their place. Not today. The ACLU fights to remove the Ten Commandments from public display—in the courthouse, the city hall, the public school. The Ten Commandments! Has the world seen a more perfect legal code than the one Moses brought down from Sinai?"

Nathan took his applause with outstretched arms—both a gesture of bafflement at what could answer this question in any but the obvious way as well as a bodybuilder's pose.

He hit successive applause points, each carefully crafted by Malcolm to lead the audience through an emotional journey culminating in the Ask and lasting fourteen and a half minutes. He practiced each sermon enough so that he moved at the teleprompter's pace and not vice versa. As a result, each sermon could be packaged to the second.

He wrapped up America as a Christian nation and moved on to the Bible as a clear moral guide, positioning God as a judge and Jesus as a teacher. Finally, with 2:10 remaining, he asked for help—first through prayers and then donations.

"I know Pastor Lloyd is looking down on us now from his place in heaven, and I know he's pleased with what he sees—millions hearing the Good News in fifty-four countries, millions digging deep to help spread the Word further still. Pastor Lloyd said, 'The bigger the need, the bigger the seed.' Your seed offering will grow thirtyfold, sixtyfold, a hundredfold, so step out in faith now. God can't multiply what you don't sow."

Nathan crescendoed the pitch and moved to his signature denouement.

"I leave it to you." His voice softened as the donation phone number slowly faded from beneath the logo. "The decision is between you and your Lord, between you and your Maker. You know your legitimate needs better than I. If you need to get that extra special present, or buy a vacation, or pay for car repairs now, that's fine. I'm sure you've chosen the right path. When you're able to sow that seed with God, we'll be here for you."

This guilt kicker had myriad variations and the donation phone lines were shut down for the last 90 seconds of the show. People who called during that time were given a polite recording that encouraged them to return during the next show. The ministry had received hundreds of messages from viewers startled and delighted that a ministry would turn down money. The loyalty of Nathan's audience was the envy of the industry.

CB

Nathan unwound after a show with low-intensity chores at his desk. The office was quieter than usual because most of the staff had left for Christmas Eve. In no rush to return to an empty house, Nathan ate a quiet lunch and used the time to clear out his email inbox and tidy his desk.

He was in the middle of reading Malcolm's press release expressing the ministry's outrage at the gay club at the high school when he heard a rap on his door.

"Nathan, got a minute?" It was the voice of Peter Baldwin, the head of merchandising.

"Sure." Nathan's focus stayed on his reading.

The door closed with a quiet click, and Nathan jerked his head up to see Peter stroll to one of the big guest chairs.

"You hit it out of the park today," Peter said as he took a seat.

"I doubt you came to talk about today's show."

"No." Peter took a piece of paper, folded lengthwise, from his inside jacket pocket. He smiled. "I just wanted to remind you of one particularly deserving employee during this season of giving." The paper flapped as he gestured.

"Nobody gets bonuses, you know that. I can't make an exception for you."

"Well, I hadn't thought of it as a bonus, but I guess you could call it that."

"What do you want? Your salary is already above the industry average."

"No, not a raise."

Nathan opened his mouth to speak but then pushed back his chair. He wouldn't participate in Peter's game.

Peter smiled. Seconds ticked by, and the smile became more forced. "Okay, here's the deal: I'm tired of scraping by."

"At 130K a year, you're hardly scraping by."

"I've got child support going to three women each month. I'm scraping by." He slapped the paper down on Nathan's desk. "And now I know how much you're *not* scraping by. I know about the Rainy Day Fund. I know how much profit this nonprofit is making."

Nathan leaned forward onto his desk.

Peter held up a hand. "You're going to say that it's all legal. Whatever—it's still embarrassing and bad for business." He picked up the paper and opened it. "170,129,000 dollars and change, spread over a number of investments. I'd list them, but it would be a waste of your time hearing something you already know all about. Here's the thing: I need a little something to help me remember the many places I put copies of," he looked down at the sheet, "rainyday.xls, so I can destroy them."

"Where did you get that?"

"Through a little snooping and some perseverance." Peter smiled again. "And Nick using his wife's birthday for a password." Nick was the accountant—good at his job but apparently not paranoid enough.

"Who have you told?"

"Not a soul. And it stays that way if I get five hundred thousand dollars. If not, I email the file to the *New York Times* and anyplace else you'd like me to add."

The fact that he had a forty-pound dumbbell next to his desk flashed through Nathan's mind. "Get out." He restrained himself from standing. This was his office. He was the boss.

Peter stood. "It's a lot to take in, I know. Think about it. Asking for a fraction of one percent of your piggy bank is quite generous on my part—consider that my gift to you. I don't need an answer immediately." The smile was back. Nathan was hating that smile. "And, Nathan, I can't imagine you'd go that far, but you may be amused to know that I have a couple of 'in the event of my death' contingencies in place. You don't want me going home to the Lord anytime soon." He pushed the folded paper across the desk. "Merry Christmas," he said as he walked out.

☙

Nathan could usually unwind in the half-hour drive to his house, but Peter's bullshit infuriated him. He drove his Mercedes S65 on the small roads like he was in a Grand Prix.

He and Janice had fallen into an unspoken division of the house. She had her bedroom suite and he had his. She used the front door and he used the back.

Nathan parked in the rear, and as he stepped out of the car, he felt dizzy. He exercised often and had to pay attention to his fluid intake. He must be dehydrated. Or maybe he was reacting to Peter.

Nathan unlocked the back door. He didn't need to turn on the light. Though the sun had set, outside lights cast bright grid patterns on the wall opposite the windows. The artwork and photos on the walls of the short hallway were the castoffs from the rest of the house and the Hundredfold offices—photos of Nathan and famous guests, a painting of an Alpine scene that had always seemed out of place, an original 1939 poster for the movie *The Wizard of Oz.* When displaced from here, they would be discarded or stored.

Nathan stopped in front of a patch of bright light that shone on Lloyd Humbert's color photo, now displaced by Nathan's in the lineup of board members, from when he had been the chair. He thought of his tribute to Lloyd on the show and felt that he had honored his old friend.

"Nate." The voice was distinct but not much louder than a whisper.

He looked around but saw no one.

"Nate." Louder now.

The voice seemed to be coming from Lloyd's photo. As he stared, the frame and the wall seemed to recede, leaving just the face, alive and staring at him. "Nate!"

"Lloyd?" Nathan felt vertigo. He needed to steady himself. He groped toward the face in the dark and touched … just a picture frame. The wall was there, and the photo, just like always. He was alone.

And clearly dehydrated. He straightened the photo and strode to the kitchen with his arms out for balance. From the refrigerator he pulled out a bottle of candy-blue electrolyte drink and drank it. He paused and looked around to make sure he was fine.

His dinner was in the refrigerator in a plastic container. The cook accommodated his need for a bodybuilder's diet, and tonight she had made grilled chicken with a fruit glaze and asparagus. His treat was an amaranth roll with flax seeds.

He put it in the microwave, took a second bottle of blue drink, and went to his office. From the back of his lower filing cabinet drawer he took a folder labeled Tough Questions.

He thumped it on his desk and stared at it. This was a worthy but unwanted adversary.

In the dining room, he set the empty drink bottle on the marble top of the Louis XIV commode. This potbellied chest of drawers was ridiculously ornate, with inlaid wood and stone, gilt bronze ornaments, and animal mouths as keyholes. He had paid 36,000 euros for it several years earlier as a gift for Janice during happier times.

He set the plastic container with his warmed dinner at the place setting at the head of the heavy dining table, also a French antique from some period he could never remember. They could seat eighteen, and Nathan by himself made for a small gathering in the grand room with its two chandeliers and red cloth wallpaper.

He ate as he leafed through the folder, a collection of handwritten notes on paper of different sizes and colors, some dating back to his early days as a serious Christian. For any other project, he would've typed it up, but computer files got archived, and older versions tended to get misplaced or overlooked. Even more than the ministry's finances, he wanted to keep this information under control.

The top sheaf of papers, held together with a paper clip, was labeled Problem of Evil. This question had taken out historian Bart Ehrman. Formerly a strong Christian, Ehrman couldn't get past the idea of an all-good god who could prevent evil in the world but didn't care to do so.

He had many pages of notes exploring the idea that evil resulted from God's gift of free will, but could God care about the free will of the murderer when he clearly didn't care about the violation to the free will of the victim? And this did nothing to resolve the problem of God creating or at least allowing natural disasters.

The next sheaf was labeled Problem of Divine Hiddenness. God demands that we come to him through Jesus, and if we don't, we burn in hell for eternity. How could this be vitally important for us to know when God won't meet us halfway by making his existence unambiguous? Why is faith necessary when that's all that a false religion would be based on?

Then the Problem of Unanswered Prayer. Jesus said that if you have faith as tiny as a mustard seed, you will be able to move mountains. Jesus said that prayer offered in faith will make the sick person well. Jesus said that whatever you ask for in prayer, believe that you have received it, and it will be yours. Jesus said that all things are possible to him who believes. Jesus said, "Whatever you ask in my name, I will do it."

But prayer didn't work that way. Earnest, selfless prayers like wishes for the improved health of a stranger might as well have never been made for all the good they did.

The image came to mind of tombstones at the top of each sheaf representing the Christians turned away from the faith by each one.

Nathan turned to the next sheaf: Why God orders genocide and condones slavery. And another: How God can be considered good when he does bad things.

Why early Judaism looks like just another Canaanite religion.

Why good and bad befall Christians no differently than any other group.

Why the Bible provides no practical scientific knowledge beyond what was known to those people at the time.

Why no medical miracles that shock science, like regrown limbs.

What role the soul has when the brain explains the mind and consciousness organically.

Why religions are not coalescing (though Christianity is a universal truth accessible by all people) but rather continuing to fragment into sects.

Why Christianity alone teaches the truth when humans throughout history have invented religions.

Why "God's plan" is in one tiny and insignificant corner of one enormous galaxy out of an inconceivably vast universe of 100 billion galaxies.

Nathan pushed away his dinner and closed the folder. Each question was an admission, a liability, a weakness. He'd delicately brought up these questions with other professionals in his field on many occasions. Once a confidante realized that he wasn't asking for Christian rationalizations but was actually struggling with the question, it was like had made some vulgar *faux pas*.

He was on his own.

CB

Nathan sat in bed with his Tough Questions folder, leafing through the topics and correcting or adding as ideas came to him. The exercise didn't relax him. He almost felt driven to pray again, but hours of prayers about these questions in years past had produced nothing but the hollow feeling that God didn't care.

He tossed the folder aside and lay back into the pillows, his palms pushed onto his eyes. This felt like one of those nights when his mind was immersed in some problem and he wouldn't sleep for hours. He went to the bathroom and took a sleeping pill. He turned off the light, flipped his pillow over to the cool side, and tried to relax.

It couldn't have been many minutes before he heard that voice again, "Nate."

Nathan switched the light back on. He opened the drawer of his nightstand and pulled out his Glock 21 handgun. It felt solid and heavy in his hand. Being comfortable with guns somehow seemed obligatory given his audience, and a .45 caliber seemed more patriotic than a nine millimeter. He now appreciated its extra stopping power.

"Nate." That was what Lloyd had called him.

But lots of people knew that. The voice came from the hallway, on the other side of his closed door. He had a clear shot of the door, and he glanced left to the window and right to the sitting room to look for intruders. He willed himself to calm down, calm down.

This had to be some kind of joke, and that would explain the voice in the entryway several hours earlier. Maybe Janice let someone in to scare him. When they saw the hardware that was staring at them, they'd change their definition of an amusing prank. If it was that SOB Peter Baldwin, he might take him out anyway, rid his life of that problem, and declare that he was shooting at an intruder.

"Nate!" That was a really good impression of Lloyd, and it seemed to be just outside the door.

Nathan racked the slide and took off the safety. "Hey, Lloyd, come on in," he said. He aimed at the door with two hands as he'd practiced at the range.

The door didn't open. Instead, a grotesque, straining face appeared on the door. It was the face from the hallway, Lloyd Humbert's face. The eyes were squeezed shut as if passing through the door demanded enormous effort. The rest of the body followed slowly, like smoke through a screen.

"You'd point a gun at your old partner?" It was Lloyd, standing in his bedroom. But it couldn't be.

"Who the hell are you?"

Lloyd was distinct but translucent—maybe a hologram? Whatever it was, the effect was quite convincing. He wore a dark gray suit, and cash peeked out of bulging jacket pockets. He held his arms as one might hold a baby, but his burden was the cheap ministry giveaways that he had pioneered—wooden cross necklaces, Jesus figurines, pocket Bibles, vials of dirt, and a dozen more. They fell from his arms as he walked closer, leaving a trail behind him like goodies scattered from a Christmas stocking, but the armload seemed to replenish, as if from a cornucopia. A noose-like prayer shawl wound tightly around his neck.

"Nate, that swearing can become a habit. Watch it."

Nathan pushed the covers aside with his left hand, the gun still aimed at Lloyd. "Get out." He stepped onto the floor and walked to the side to view the phantom from a different angle.

Lloyd stared back, the face still slightly contorted, saying nothing.

"I said, get out."

"Nate, I'm here to talk to you. The gun doesn't help, and I have little time."

Nathan's outstretched hand collapsed into a fist. The gun was gone. He felt vulnerable and took a step back. "Who are you?"

"I am what I seem to be."

"You seem to be a trick."

"Be still and listen to me. I was successful in the ministry game, and you were a great partner. We pulled in millions, but we did nothing useful with it. We spent it on distribution and consultants and equipment—we spent money only to make more money.

"And to feather our nests." Lloyd looked around Nathan's grand bedroom suite. "What a waste to have had such resources but done nothing to address mankind's problems."

"We gave to a lot of charities." Nathan had to stand up for himself.

"Investments—all of them. Who do you think you're talking to? We chose those charities together. Seven percent of our revenue went to good works, and even that had lots of missionary overhead."

Nathan was about to say, "It's eight percent now," but instead said, "Missionaries do good work."

"Starving people need more food, not more Bibles." In life, Lloyd had always shown an inexhaustible confidence no matter the challenge, but his face now bore the pain of some inner torment. "I'm paying the price for my selfishness, but you may yet avoid my fate. You will be tested, starting tonight. You will have three visitors."

"Visitors? Who, exactly?"

"Whoever you need. I'm your friend, Nathan. Take my advice and make the most of this. Learn what you must learn."

The giveaways stopped spilling from Lloyd's arms, and he appeared to have stopped, too. Nathan stepped to the side to get a better look. Lloyd seemed to be frozen and perhaps more transparent.

"Lloyd?"

No response.

"Lloyd, we need to talk. I think I'll give the test a pass if you don't mind."

The immobile figure continued to dim.

"Lloyd!" Nathan was alone.

He put on his bathrobe and walked around the bed and the perimeter of the room, looking for anything amiss. The trinkets that had littered the floor were gone. He opened the nightstand drawer. The Glock was there.

"Oh, Jesus." It wasn't much of a prayer, but it was more than he usually said. Nathan lay on the bed, suddenly very tired.

Second Stanza

Nathan heard a female voice.

"Nathan, wake up."

He opened his eyes. He'd been asleep, and the crazy memories of Lloyd flooded back. What had he dreamed, and what had been real?

Unfamiliar light illuminated his bedroom. He sat up and saw, in the space between the door and his bed where Lloyd had been, a glowing person. A familiar person.

"Sophia?" It certainly looked like Sophia, though instead of her usual frumpy clothes she wore a sort of toga with a rope belt, and her feet were bare. Her skin and clothes were almost white, as if she were a Greek marble statue. The light that filled the room seemed to come mostly from her head, though her whole body glowed white.

"I only look like someone you know," the ghost said, in Sophia's voice. "You can call me Wisdom if you'd like, though actually my title is the Accuser."

Nathan didn't like the sound of that. "Why are you here?"

"For your benefit."

"What are you going to do to me?"

Wisdom took a step backwards and beckoned him with two fingers. Nathan felt a force push him out of bed, like a strong wind that affected only him.

He stood and followed Wisdom as she turned and walked to the sitting room. As they faced the drape-covered windows, she touched his hand, and the wall vanished.

They were now in a large noisy room full of busy children. Bright sun shone on snow outside the window. Looking down at himself, he realized he still wore only pajamas and bathrobe. His bare feet touched a hard linoleum floor, though it didn't feel cold. "What are we doing here?" he whispered to Wisdom. "I'm not dressed."

"No one can see or hear us."

"Where are we?"

"You tell me."

Nathan looked again at the room, the children, and several adults who seemed to be teachers. *It can't be.* "I went to camp here." He looked to Wisdom for confirmation. "I went to camp during Christmas vacation because my parents had to work. Look, there's Brad Pemberton, and there's Tommy Williams." Nathan took a step closer to one table. "Oh, Jesus. And there's me."

The boy that caught Nathan's attention had short hair and ears that stuck out. He stood with a number of other children, all perhaps eight years old, directing the others as they uncovered bones buried in a sandbox.

"Young Nathan looks happy," Wisdom said.

"And why not? I loved this place. I went here for years at Christmas, and it was always my best present."

"You wanted to be an archeologist."

"And then a doctor and then a physicist, but at this age, it was archeology. It looks like we were uncovering a miniature Tyrannosaur this time." Nathan walked closer to the children and watched for a minute, feeling again the childhood thrill of discovery and learning. "We grew seeds in a drinking glass so you could see the roots. We used microscopes to see what was in puddle water and telescopes to look at distant trees. We built bridges from straws and tape, and we grew crystals from sugar water. This place taught me to question, to enjoy learning new things." He paused a second to catch his breath. "We learned just for the joy of it."

He wondered about the physics in this strange world and reached out to touch the table. His hand went through, though he appeared just as opaque as the children. He touched himself—solid. He wondered if Wisdom was solid as well—she certainly looked it.

"You're still a scientist," Wisdom said, "in everything except science."

"What does that mean?"

" 'When science and scripture clash, you gonna trust man or God?' I believe you said that recently." His words sounded strange in her mouth, like it was evidence presented in a courtroom.

"You just don't understand my industry."

The spirit said nothing. With the first two fingers of her right hand she touched Nathan's shoulder.

Nathan looked around—now they were in the kitchen of a modest house with low ceilings. Christmas decorations, worn and familiar, sat on the table. In a corner of the adjacent family room stood a small Christmas tree adorned with lights, decorations, and lead tinsel and with a skirt made of a white sheet.

"I grew up here," Nathan said, turning to see everything. "This was my house. I made that bowl. There's my father's fishing rod." He pointed as he strode around, taking it all in. "And smell that! My mother baked a pie."

The front door down the hall opened, and the three of them walked in—young Nathan, about twelve this time, and his parents, looking healthy and energetic. They were younger than he was now, probably twenty years younger. Nathan had never given more than an idle thought to them as young adults, and yet here they stood, right in front of him. He had last seen his mother at a nursing home a month earlier, her mind vacant from Alzheimer's, and his father had died years before while Nathan was still young.

"Nate, hang up your suit."

"Okay, Mom." Little Nate took off his jacket as he walked to the door to the basement.

Wisdom gestured that they should follow.

"I hated that suit," Nathan said as he followed his younger self down the stairs. "We must've just come home from church." The air was damp and smelled faintly of detergent and chemicals.

In a corner of the basement, near a bright fluorescent light, Nate fiddled with the tiny hose on an air pump. Shelves to the side held his science supplies: a collection of crystals, a chemistry set from two birthdays earlier, and boxes of cool things that might be useful someday: the copper wire unwound from an old motor, prisms and lenses, gears, colored light filters, a compass, a solar cell. His collection of a dozen science books had been bought from the castoffs bin at a university library.

"You were always working on something," Wisdom said.

"It was hydroponics at this point." Under the light, about twenty slender plants poked through cotton batting on top of a narrow plastic trough. A faint bubbling sound came from the trough. "Growing plants without dirt fascinated me."

Wisdom pointed to Nate's Bible on the table on top of his suit jacket. "But church didn't."

"Scratchy suits and meaningless church services—no, it didn't seem important to me then. It was just what we did, like pledge allegiance to the flag or eat turkey at Thanksgiving. We were Baptists. I was so immersed that it didn't occur to me to question. I knew who was in our community and who went to a different church. I knew which of my friends and relatives were going to heaven and which were going to hell."

"Friends going to hell? That's a lot to burden a child with."

"I never thought of it that way. Religion to me was like water to a fish. But I do remember being startled awake a couple of times by some noise and thinking that this was it—this was the end, this was Armageddon. What about my Catholic friends, my Jewish friends, my uncle Frank who was an atheist? I prayed for them every night, though that never seemed to do anything."

"Did prayer ever work?"

"I tracked my prayers, like an experiment—both the general ones like peace in the Middle East and specific ones like recovery for sick members of the church. I even had a control group—other wishes I didn't pray for. Some things happened, and some didn't, and whether I prayed or not made no apparent difference."

"You seem to have made your peace with prayer. You use it often on your show."

Prayer is effective when donations come along with it, Nathan thought.

☙

Wisdom touched Nathan's arm, and the basement dissolved away like icing rinsed from a window. They were outdoors, and Nathan blinked in the strong sun. They stood in a large field—no, the quad at a university. Bare trees lined the sidewalk, and young people walked by, dressed for cold weather. In front of them, three young men threw a red Frisbee.

And over there, that was Baker House, his residence during his freshman year in college. It must be the end of his first semester, maybe that euphoric period after exams. He considered the three Frisbee players, looking for a familiar face.

Sure enough. "That's Eric Seibert. We were both physics majors. The guy was brilliant. He won the department prize for outstanding senior project. I wonder what happened to him. He had a lot of promise."

"So did you. You turned your back on a successful career. You could've gotten your doctorate. Maybe a professorship."

Nathan occasionally thought about this road not taken. He was in the elite ranks of his field as a televangelist, but in these circles, his scientific past would be an embarrassment, a youthful indiscretion. A career in physics would've been different in almost every way. Nevertheless, he came at televangelism with a different approach than his competition, and his analytical mind drove his success. He could dismantle or step out of the way of problems that stymied some of his dimwitted rivals who relied on faith. Nathan considered their mindless approach to be like using a hammer to slice bread. Faith to solve real-world problems was simply not the right tool.

He thought for a moment about this spirit guide. Ever since she had dragged him out of bed, he had no trouble distinguishing her from Sophia, despite the resemblance. Competent but timid Sophia was not like this confident and seemingly omniscient leader.

He looked at her and wondered what she wore, if anything, under her toga. She turned to him with a hint of a glower, and he drove the thought from his mind and turned back to the three students.

"And that's Gary ... Gary Sutton."

"You were his only friend at this time."

"Gary needed one. He came out as gay when he got to college, which was a bad move. This was the late seventies. It wasn't like it is now. Some students made it their mission to harass him, and it was tempting to join in. My upbringing strongly rejected homosexuality, but it also demanded helping people in need." He turned toward Wisdom. "Do you know what happened to him?"

"We're here to focus on your past." She pointed to the third figure, the closest one, who turned to catch a Frisbee from behind.

"It's me—and with that stupid beard. And I could lose a good thirty pounds."

"Let's look at another Christmas season." Wisdom pointed behind them and Nathan turned.

They were in a small classroom now, half full with about thirty students. They spoke in turn, their voices echoing in the bare room. Nathan knew the room well. This was a Calvin Fellowship in Christ meeting, and Nathan had spent many pleasant hours in such gatherings of this Christian club. Meeting activities ranged from social gatherings and personal testimonials to discussions of apologetics and theology.

He scanned the backs of the students looking for old friends.

"You came to this group seeking something."

"I joined in my senior year. My father had died over the summer. I came for answers—and solace."

"And something else."

"I'd fallen away from the church during college. It seemed irrelevant. That disappointed my parents, my father in particular. He made it clear during his last days that he wanted me back in. A dying wish is hard to ignore."

"Would your father be pleased to see you now?"

Nathan was at the top of his game as a televangelist. He was one of the world's most successful preachers, both in reach and in revenue. There were just a handful of active preachers who rivaled him.

He looked away.

☙

The college scene dissolved into another gathering, a full congregation in a small church with uneven white plaster walls and dark wooden beams. Four lit candles filled an advent wreath on the table at the front. Polished brass wall sconces with candles, decorated for the season with holly full of bright red berries, were prominent along the walls.

Nathan leaned over. "New Life Church," he whispered. "This building was built before the Civil War." He and a few other young idealists had helped restart a dying church shortly after college.

"One more announcement," the preacher said. "Someone left a glass casserole dish last Sunday. You can pick it up from the buffet table in the basement. And now it's time for our financial report for the year."

He remembered the preacher—one of the young elders who, like himself, took turns leading the service.

The preacher summarized the church's finances—where every dollar came from and where it went. Nothing was allocated for salaries since volunteers filled every job. "This is our second year, and our second year in the black. We have a surplus of 920 dollars, so bring to the Christmas party your ideas for whom to give that to. Let's see whose Christmas we can make a little brighter."

Wisdom dismissed the project with a wave. "They take it all so seriously, like it's hard. They pay no staff or satellite transmission fees. They have no market share to worry about. They don't know what hard is."

"No—*this* was real ministering. We really helped people." Nathan hadn't thought about this gulf in a long time. "It's not like that anymore." He looked around at the people who made this congregation live. His Hundredfold studio, full of cameras, spotlights, and crew, was irreconcilably different from this historic church.

Perhaps his younger self was in the congregation. He walked down a side aisle. The third pew from the front, on the right side—that was where he usually sat. And there he was, probably twenty-five years old, and next to him, someone else. "I forgot how pretty she was," he said, almost to himself, about the young woman next to him. She was his wife, Becky Thorpe. How lucky he had been. In the potluck of life, she was the angel food cake amid the green Jell-O.

Becky wore a long-sleeved blue dress that almost reached her ankles. With a bonnet, she would've looked like a Mennonite. She preferred old-fashioned dresses for church, and they seemed to fit her to this church more perfectly.

He had met Becky in the Calvin Fellowship group in college, and they married just after graduation. Looking back on his younger self, married life had been marvelous and magical, like being in a toy store.

"Here's a meeting that was important to your career." Wisdom pointed behind. Though Nathan wanted to linger, he turned and saw his younger self in Lloyd Humbert's office. This would've been one of his first meetings with Lloyd, when he was about twenty-eight. He had shifted his career from physics to ministry some years earlier.

Lloyd was in his forties, tall, jovial, and confident, and he was vastly more experienced and knowledgeable than Nathan. Lloyd had a large church, and his sermons were broadcast on a local TV station. His reach and income was now greater from the TV audience than from his church. Lloyd was deciding what to do about this opportunity.

Young Nathan said to Lloyd, "But a prayer can't inform God of something he doesn't already know, and it makes no sense to ask God to deviate from what he knows is best."

Lloyd said, "A good prayer is of the form, 'Lord, help me to understand your plan' or 'Conform me to your plan.' "

"That makes sense, but it's not what the Bible promises. John says, 'Ask for anything in my name, and I will do it.' Matthew says, 'If you believe, you will receive what you ask for in prayer.' James says, 'The prayer offered in faith will make the sick person well.' "

"Prayers of petition are just one kind," Lloyd said. "There are others—prayers of thanksgiving, prayers of confession, prayers of praise."

"But even the Lord's Prayer has a petition, 'Give us this day our daily bread.' "

Lloyd held up his hands. "I have no answer. One of the Christian's burdens is mystery—why God supports genocide and slavery in the Old Testament, why the Bible seems to contradict itself, why prayer doesn't work as advertised. But don't let that stop you asking the questions that need answers. Too few Christians do. You're a Christian with the mind of a scientist—we need more of those."

As the two men continued to talk, Wisdom said, "Have you resolved these issues?"

"No. They still frustrate me."

"What took you to Lloyd?" Wisdom asked.

"I had taken on the job of pastor at the church. The church was just big enough by then to support a fulltime pastor, but it was hard living. We probably got half our income as food—extra vegetables from someone's garden, a frozen meatloaf, or leftovers from the Sunday brunch. Becky took it all cheerfully. She seemed made for a life of giving, but I wanted more.

"Anyway, as pastor, I had to answer the difficult questions from church members, and I didn't have anything but rationalizations for the toughest ones, so I asked Lloyd for help. He was a local celebrity, and he surprised me by giving me his time. A short chat became a weekly discussion, which became a partnership. I became the manager of his television show."

"But more than just parishioners asked the questions."

"Yes, some came from me. I realized that I believed because I was raised that way. If I'd been born in India, I'd have been a Hindu; in Saudi Arabia, a Muslim. I began reading not just Christian apologetics but also atheist literature. There I was, a new pastor with responsibility over a congregation, learning new ways to undercut the Christian message. It felt wrong somehow."

"Then why do it?"

"If Christianity is true, it should be able to stand up to inquiry. I should be able to discard what it says, like Euclid's postulates, and rediscover the truth, right?"

"And did you rediscover Christianity's truth?"

"Through faith, yes, but that wasn't what I wanted. I'd hoped to support the claims of Christianity with reason, but I've never found that foundation to be solid. It was time to go all in or fold, and I was in too far to back out. Living with a Christianity that didn't pass the tests of truth that I applied to everything else felt better than turning my back on the life I'd made for myself. And coming into Lloyd's orbit made it easier to ignore these annoying issues and operate on faith. He had a strong personality and great rationalizations."

Lloyd's office faded, replaced by a big, empty kitchen. Cardboard moving boxes were stacked in some corners, and flattened boxes leaned in others. Becky stood in front of a wide white counter, putting silverware from a box into a white drawer. White cabinet doors stood open below the row of drawers and above the counter.

Nathan walked in. "How do you like the kitchen?" His voice echoed in the hollow house.

"It's like an operating room."

"It's huge. What is it—four times bigger than the one in the apartment?"

"We made do with the old one."

"But now we have nothing to be embarrassed about. We can be proud to have people over."

Becky's face clouded, and she looked away.

"Oh, not this again. Look—I did this for you. You deserved more than that crappy apartment."

"Don't tell me you did this for me," she said through sobs. "This was all for you—the job with Lloyd, the new car, this house. Your beliefs are harder now, not welcoming. You sold your soul. I don't even recognize you with all the time you spend in the gym and the tanning place."

"I'm trying to make a new career. I'm trying to be a good provider. We want to have kids, right? I'm sorry you're unimpressed with my efforts."

"I *am* impressed—hours at the gym and eating nothing but chicken and chemicals, working so hard at your job—but I liked your old job. Ministering to people in need suited you. The money would've come with time. Or maybe it wouldn't. I don't care. You're changing your theology based on what sells. You're just a piece in a machine."

"In time, perhaps the television face of a big ministry. My impact is already much more than I could've imagined."

"It's just television. I loved our little church, with people you could actually touch."

"I'm not going through this again. I can't reason with you." Nathan walked out.

Becky turned away. With her hands gripping the edge of the sink, she looked out the window as tears ran down her face. She seemed so fragile.

Wisdom looked at Nathan but said nothing.

Nathan felt a bit like the accused in a courtroom, hearing the charges read out against him. He began a defense in his mind, but he had very little to argue with. "I've wondered what it would've been like if we'd done it her way," Nathan said as he watched Becky cry. "Small church pastor, raising a family on rice and beans, turning down celebrity jobs. Hard to imagine. I'm suited to the high profile life. But if I could, I know I'd make one change."

"Janice," Wisdom said.

Frustrated at the rift between he and Becky after the move to Lloyd's television ministry, Nathan had focused on work and, in particular, on one of the singers in Lloyd's studio. He was looking for comfort, and Janice had been willing to provide it. Becky found out, and, after some halfhearted attempts at reform, Becky and he divorced five years after they were married.

Thinking back on it, Nathan was surprised that, of the many strong feelings he experienced during that time—love, lust, anger, hurt, guilt—irony wasn't one of them. He was a public Christian, on display as an example to all, and he had hurt someone after justifying it through shallow rationalization. On television, he had all the answers, and yet he was among the worst sinners. True, he hadn't murdered anyone, but that was small solace.

ଓ

"Let's look at a happier scene." Wisdom pointed, and before them appeared a Norman Rockwell Christmas. A group of more than a dozen people of all ages sat in a dining room around a dining table too large for the room. The table overflowed with the usual Christmas bounty—turkey, dressing, gravy, cranberry sauce, rolls, mashed potatoes, vegetables—and the air held their warm smells. A selection of pies sat on the sideboard.

The diners chatted and laughed, and silverware clinked on the china. Nathan scanned for familiar faces. "Luna—there's my sister Luna. And next to her, that must be Margaret her daughter. She's just a teenager—this must be ten years ago. I don't recognize anyone else."

"Luna's in-laws." Wisdom gestured to the two ends of the long table. "Her husband." She pointed again. "And the rest are family." After a pause, she said, "It's nice having family to visit on holidays."

"I have Christmas plans," Nathan blurted out, a little faster than he intended.

"I never said you didn't."

In truth, Nathan planned on spending Christmas alone. He would probably fix his Christmas dinner from the pantry. Maybe he'd do some weights in the garage. Maybe he'd have an extra roll as a treat.

"Your sister dropped out of your life," Wisdom said. "Or did you push her out?"

"She pushed me out. My Christianity offended her somehow. And then she envied my lifestyle, which I'll admit is a bit extravagant, but that doesn't give her any claim to it."

"She asked for money?"

"Not in so many words," Nathan said, "but I can take a hint. They can't be living on much. She's a social worker, and I believe her husband is a music teacher."

"That's right."

"She has a computer science degree from MIT. She was the CTO of a startup."

"She changed careers to have more time for her daughter."

"That's a huge sacrifice."

"Parents do that."

The conversation at the table continued, sometimes a single story or reminiscence and other times breaking into several parallel discussions, like a river that braids around islands for a stretch and then returns to a single channel.

Nathan stepped to the side to get a better view of his family. Luna was probably about forty. Laughing and talking, she seemed completely comfortable here and fully welcomed. She was part of a family. The scene touched him in ways he didn't expect. He blinked.

Wisdom turned to him. "Are you crying?"

"No, no. Nothing."

"Are you sure? I thought you were crying."

"Are we done?"

Wisdom paused, looking up at Nathan. "Not quite," she said. "Let's see them the next morning."

In moments the scene faded into darkness and back to full daylight. They were still in the dining room, but the Christmas dinner was gone and sunlight streamed in the window. The table was smaller—extra leaves must have been taken out—and it had chairs and placemats for six. Luna and Margaret sat on one side, alone in the room, with empty breakfast plates in front of them.

"Did you hear about the earthquake?" Luna said.

"No—where was it?" Margaret was engaged in something on her phone.

"Somewhere in the Indian Ocean near Indonesia. And there was a tsunami. It might've killed tens of thousands of people."

Margaret put down the phone.

"It happened last night while we were having dinner," Luna said. "It was thirty feet high when it came ashore—I can't image. That's the kind of thing that makes you count your blessings." She leaned over and kissed Margaret on the head.

"What an unhappy Christmas present," Margaret said.

"I doubt many celebrate Christmas in that part of the world, but I know what you mean."

"How would Christians explain this? If it were something good, like a war ending or a drought ending or even a plane crash where no one died, they'd say that God did it, especially if it happened now, at Christmas. So what do they say when something bad happens?"

Luna paused. "We all interpret the facts so that they support our world view. Christians do it, but we have to watch out for that in ourselves. We want to understand the facts as they are, not as we wish they were. On the positive side, religious people often have community. That's something that can have real value. If someone dealing with catastrophe gets comfort from spiritual beliefs, who am I to complain? I hope I'm never able to speak from experience about what that feels like."

"If God won't help, we should," Margaret said.

"That's my girl." Luna gave her a hug.

☙

Wisdom pointed behind her, and Nathan turned. Here again, Nathan didn't recognize the location. They were in a modest living room crowded with functional though not stylish furniture. A fire burned in the fireplace beneath a mantle holding a nativity scene and four stockings, and a hint of campfire smell filled the room. A Christmas tree filled one corner, and a man sat reading on the couch. The man looked a little younger than Nathan, maybe fifty, and Nathan didn't recognize him.

"Merry Christmas." It was Becky's voice. She walked into the living room, probably twenty years older than before, but she was unmistakable and still attractive.

"Before I forget," the man said, "I heard news about an old friend of yours today."

Becky smiled as she stood in front of the fire. Nathan missed that smile.

The man said, "Remember Lloyd Humbert, the Hundred-fold Ministries guy? He just died. Nathan Thorpe is set to take the top spot."

The smile faded, and Becky slowly looked down. "Nathan will finally get what he's wanted all these years. I hope it makes him happy."

Nathan tried to read her expression—compassion maybe, or sympathy? What he didn't see was regret for her having rejected that path.

Becky smoothed down the back of her dress, warm from the fire. "Santa needs to get out the presents. I'm reading to the kids." She walked over and kissed the man and then strode up the stairs.

Wisdom gestured that they should follow.

At the top of the stairs, Nathan walked to an open door and peeked in. Becky lay on a bed with a girl of about twelve on one side and a boy of about eight on the other. From the toys on the floor and desk, he guessed that this was the boy's room.

" 'Twas the night before Christmas," Becky read from the book in her lap in a solemn voice.

"Becky certainly seems to have gotten what she wanted," Nathan said.

"She got what she strove for," Wisdom said. "So did you."

Nathan had indeed gotten the brass ring, though he wasn't sure anymore that it was worth what he paid for it.

They watched as Becky finished reading the Christmas poem to her children. The children seemed too excited to sleep, and they talked about their favorite Christmas memories.

Nathan turned to Wisdom. "What happened to Eric? I lost track after he went to grad school."

"He got his doctorate in physics and became a professor. He was a pioneer in the field of ferrofluids. He's married with two boys on their own. Now he teaches science in a high school."

"Doesn't sound like much money in that."

"He loves his work. Isn't that enough?"

"What about Gary? We lost touch after freshman year."

"He had some issues in his later college years. Your friendship meant a lot to him. You may not have been paying attention to him, but he paid attention to you. You backtracked on your support for gay rights after you joined Calvin Fellowship in Christ in your senior year."

"Oh that. That was just what they did. The group was anti-gay, so I had to be. My position was like a club tie—just something to justify membership in the group."

"To you it may have been a harmless fashion statement, but it was a big deal to Gary. He admired you, and your rejection of who he was carried a lot of weight. He tried acting straight, and when that became too big a burden, he tried suicide. He endured a rough couple of years—gay conversion therapy, depression, he even considered electroshock therapy."

"Oh, God, I had no idea. That wasn't the intention. It was supposed to be about love and forgiveness of sin."

"And homosexuals loving who they're attracted to is sinful? Judging people has consequences."

"Where is he now?"

"He's an accountant in Los Angeles, and he's doing well. He accepts who he is and has been in a relationship for close to ten years."

Becky arranged the covers on the boy and kissed him on the forehead. "Good night, little mister. I love you."

"I love you, too, Mom."

As Becky walked out holding her daughter's hand, Nathan thought of what might have been. Family had always wound up as a second-tier priority, with no time even to satisfy first-tier priorities. At this stage in life, as he began to feel his mortality, it would've been nice to have someone call him "Dad."

Wisdom put her hand on Nathan's shoulder, and he found himself back in bed, alone.

Third Stanza

Nathan jerked awake as if dreaming he'd fallen off a cliff. His bedroom was lit again, though not with Wisdom's pale light. Now it was more like the intense spotlights in his production studio.

Another ghost? Lloyd had warned him of three. Nathan sat up and saw that the light came from the sitting room. His bedroom connected to the sitting room with double doors, one of which was open, and a blaze of light poured through. The thought burst upon Nathan's sleepy brain that maybe the room was *ablaze*. He threw off the covers and ran to the door, shielding his eyes with one arm.

"Is anyone there? What's going on?"

Nathan squinted in the bright light. There didn't seem to be any specific light source. Instead, the room was just … bright, as if the intensity of everything was somehow amplified. On the couch against the wall sat a man. A really large man. He was probably nine or ten feet tall. Nathan quickly approximated how his own weight would scale up and guessed the man to be about a thousand pounds. And this was a linebacker-fit thousand pounds. He wore light gray dress pants with cuffs and a tight-fitting sky blue tank top. With biceps like footballs, he was ripped enough to be on the cover of a muscle magazine. The giant was black with a shaved head and looked to be in his thirties, but the most surprising thing about him was his enthusiastic grin. He took off his sunglasses and said, "Come in and know me better, man!" The cheerful voice fit the body. It was loud and deep.

"Are you another Accuser?" Nathan said.

"No need for formalities—call me Jim."

Nathan looked at this colossus, cautiously optimistic because of the jovial expression but still unsure of how afraid he should be. He looked like a demigod or superhero, though Nathan was pretty sure that superheroes wore spandex, not this confused cross between board room and weight room. "Are you one of the Nephilim?"

The ghost slapped the couch and laughed. "Black dude as a 'son of God'? Not in *your* Bible!" He stood from the couch with a quick and graceful motion, confirming Nathan's comparison with a linebacker, and put his baseball mitt of a hand on Nathan's shoulder as if Nathan were a nine-year-old kid brother. The sitting room fell away.

☙

They were now in a small kitchen. Sophia stirred a pot while her daughter Kay slowly arranged marshmallows on top of a dish of yams. Potpourri boiled on the back of the stove, and Nathan could smell turkey, too. Christmas dishes covered the countertops—stuffing, gravy, rolls, and a red cylinder of cranberry sauce.

"I wanted colored pencils for Christmas," Kay said.

Kay seemed about fourteen now. Nathan had met Sophia's husband and daughter before, but staying up to date with the employees' personal lives had never been a priority.

"We've been over that," Sophia said. "You still have lots of crayons."

"Those are for little kids."

"We just couldn't afford any more presents this year." Sophia came over to look at Kay's project. "Did you finish putting the marshmallows on? How many fit?"

"Nine rows, with six in each."

"And how many is that? What's nine times six?"

"Fifty … six?"

"Fifty-four. Now offset the rows like I showed you to make a honeycomb pattern, and see if more fit on."

As Kay rearranged the marshmallows, Sophia said, "It's almost one o'clock. Do you remember who's coming for dinner today?" Together, they went through the list—Sophia's sister Jeannie, her husband, and two kids; the grandmother on Sophia's side; and the family from down the street with their two kids. "Everyone will be so happy to see you, now that you're out of the hospital."

Nathan turned to Jim, bent down to avoid the ceiling. "That's a lot of people."

"Larry behaves better in a crowd."

Nathan was about to ask about the hospital when a gravely male voice came from outside the kitchen. "Sophia! I need a beer." Nathan heard a television with some sports event elsewhere in the house.

Sophia pulled the pot off the stove, strode to the refrigerator, and pulled out a can of soda. "Kay, I think Daddy's had enough beer for now. Take him this." She opened the can, handed it to Kay, and pushed her out of the kitchen. Sophia stepped away from the doorway, bowed her head, and reached up to touch the frame of a needlepointed sampler of Psalm 23:4 hanging on the wall. "Yea, though I walk through the valley of the shadow of death, I will fear no evil." Her lips silently mouthed a prayer.

Kay came back, still holding the can. "Daddy wants you, and he's mad."

Sophia pushed Kay back to the counter and her marsh-mallow project. "I need you to finish this. Listen to me: you stay here in the kitchen."

"I'm scared."

"It'll be fine." She gave Kay a hug, then took a can of beer from the refrigerator and opened it as she walked.

Nathan followed her out of the kitchen, across the dining room, and into the family room. Larry sat on a worn blue couch in front of a too-loud television showing a bowl game. He looked uncomfortably dressy in khakis, loafers without socks, and a polo shirt not quite long enough to cover his round hairy belly. His curly black hair extended along his face as bushy sideburns.

"I'm sorry, Larry. Here's your beer." Sophia held out the can.

Larry looked up from the couch and slowly got to his feet. He was no taller than Sophia, though much heavier, and he adjusted his feet as if he were a statesman settling himself before beginning an address. Or a boxer about to begin a workout on a punching bag.

He smacked the can out of Sophia's hand. It bounced off the wall and hissed out foam onto the carpet where it landed.

Nathan was startled by the quick move. He looked at the splash mark on the wall and saw similar stains on the wall and carpet. The room had a war-torn look, with decorative plates glued together and chips in the coffee table and sideboard. The walls had their own scars, some filled with white plaster and some left alone.

"I asked for a beer, and you sent me a Coke. What should you have given me?"

"A beer."

"Yes, a beer." He punctuated the "yes" with a slap—another surprisingly quick movement.

"Larry, please—not today." Sophia tipped her head down and shielded the sides of her head with her arms so that her elbows pointed forward.

"I won't be disrespected in my own house." Larry smacked at her head, moving around to avoid her arms.

"It's Christmas, Larry." Sophia's voice was muffled.

"I don't give a goddamn what day it is—you'll respect me and do what you're told." Slaps turned to punches.

Nathan pushed Jim. "Go—do something."

"You know how this works. We're observers."

Nathan had the Hulk by his side, and yet he wouldn't do anything. "Don't you care?"

Jim waved his hand through the sideboard as if it were a hologram.

Nathan paced around the drunken fool as he kept slapping Sophia, unable to do anything. "Run away!" he said to Sophia, and then to Jim, "Why does she stand her ground?"

"If he spends his energy on her, Kay is safe."

Finally a new sound, that of Sophia sobbing. Larry seemed to wake from a trance, or perhaps this had been his goal all along. Like a cat that falls and then licks its paws as if nothing happened, Larry stepped back, surveyed his work, sagged back into the couch, and turned his interest back to the television. "And clean up this mess," he said.

Sophia ran to Kay, hugged her, and ran upstairs, whimpering as she went.

"How often does this happen?" Nathan said as he watched the loathsome pig sit and watch his game.

"How often does she wear a scarf to work?"

"Is that why she does that?"

"Bruises on her body are easier to hide. Bruises to the spirit never heal completely."

"Why does she put up with it?"

" 'Wives, submit yourselves to your husbands.' I think you've preached on that one."

"This isn't what I meant."

"Doesn't much matter what you meant if this is how it's interpreted. Both Sophia and Larry see this kind of submission as obligatory."

Sophia returned downstairs wearing a scarf and a long-sleeved sweater. She trotted into the kitchen and then returned to the family room, leaving a can of beer, picking up the empty one from the carpet, and blotting up the spill with a dishcloth.

Without acknowledgment or apology or even a glance in Sophia's direction, Larry opened the can.

Nathan and Jim followed Sophia back into the kitchen, where she resumed her cooking. She tried to rekindle some Christmas spirit, but Kay was subdued. Sophia turned on a radio to a station playing Christmas carols.

Minutes later, the doorbell rang, and Kay ran to the front door. "Aunt Jeannie!"

"Kay, it's great to see you so strong after the hospital."

"It was almost two weeks this time."

"You're so brave." Jeannie gave Kay a hug, followed by a man Kay addressed as Uncle Ken.

Nathan said, "Why was she in the hospital?"

"She's been in eight times. The prognosis for her heart condition isn't good."

"Can it be fixed?"

"There is an operation, but they can't afford it."

"But they can afford eight hospital stays?"

"You don't have to pay if you come in through the emergency room."

The two children ran off with Kay as Sophia came to the door.

Sophia's sister touched the scarf. "Oh, no—did that bastard hit you again? On Christmas?"

"Jeannie, not now. It's easiest to just let it go."

"There's no excuse."

"He got laid off again."

"Fired, more likely." Jeannie hugged her and whispered, "You know that you and Kay are welcome to stay with us and we'd keep you safe."

"I've told you that I can't do that, but thank you."

"Good Christian wives need to use common sense as well as the Bible."

Nathan said, "Doesn't she ever think of leaving that jerk?"

" 'What God has joined together, let no one separate.' You've preached on that as well. These aren't empty words to her. Though it's hard to understand, she trusts you completely. I hope you take that trust seriously."

Other guests arrived after Jeannie and Ken, first Sophia's mother and then the neighbor family. Larry called out to the men as they arrived, encouraged some holiday cheer on them and took a few drinks for himself, and invited them to watch the game. The women had brought food to contribute to dinner and helped Sophia in the kitchen.

Nathan said, "How does dinner play out? Does Larry behave?"

"Depends on what you mean by 'behave,' but he's not violent. He carves the turkey like he was the founder of the feast, even though he's been out of a job for a month and has never been the primary breadwinner. He's annoyed that Sophia's relatives are here but his aren't within driving distance, and he criticizes the dishes everyone brought. He slurs his speech and falls asleep in front of the television after dinner, which pleases everyone.

"Sophia's scarf and sweater are the elephant in the room for her sister and mother. They know that Larry has become violent again, which is usually because he's drinking, which is usually because he's lost his job again. And Sophia compares Kay with the other kids. Kay is the oldest, but Sophia knows that the other children are already passing her cognitively. Sophia has made her peace with Kay's mental condition. She knows that Kay may never live independently. She knows she won't share the milestones that mothers typically share with their children—careers, marriage, babies. But the one thing she won't make peace with is Kay's health. The other kids might live to be ninety, but the doctors say Kay will be lucky to make it to adulthood."

Nathan said, "And what do you say? Will she live?"

For once the ghost paused, as if giving this information might break some sort of spiritual regulation. "Without the operation, she will not. Three Christmases from now, Kay will be only a beloved memory. Sophia will be too old for more children, and she will see her future as little more than bondage. But that's God's perfect plan, right? We rejoice that God has done what's best for us. That's what you told Sophia when she was pregnant. At a fork in the road, where she could've opted to be like these other two mothers, you demanded that she take this path."

Nathan looked at Sophia, a strong woman in a difficult situation, wise enough to do what was best for her daughter. He had prevented her from choosing a brighter future before understanding or even considering what he'd condemned her to.

❧

With his big hand on Nathan's shoulder, Jim turned him around. Nathan found himself in another family room, this one shared by an old couple. A man sat in a chair with an afghan on his lap, and a woman sat knitting on a couch. Needlepointed Bible verses hung on the walls, and the wallpaper was peeling in places. A small fake Christmas tree with tiny colored lights sat in a corner. In front of it, a small grocery bag was stuffed with torn wrapping paper.

No potpourri here—the place smelled moldy and stagnant. The couple was watching the television, which was too loud.

"Should I know these people?" Nathan said.

"They know you." Jim pointed at the television.

They were watching Nathan's show, the one he had recorded that day.

From the television, the voice blared, "I know Pastor Lloyd is looking down on us now from his place in heaven, and I know he's pleased with what he sees." Nathan considered his image and noted that he looked a bit too scolding. "Pastor Lloyd said, 'The bigger the need, the bigger the seed.' Your seed offering will grow thirtyfold, sixtyfold, a hundredfold, so step out in faith now. God can't multiply what you don't sow."

Jim nudged Nathan. "If it rhymes, it must be true, right? Watch this next bit. You'll love it."

The woman turned down the volume and picked up the telephone. She squinted at the television image every few digits as she dialed. "I'd like to make a donation," she said.

It was a laborious conversation, but Nathan's telephone staff was selected for their patience. He prided himself on his good customer service.

The woman initially offered a twenty dollar donation. After a slow-motion enumeration of her name, address, and credit card number, Jim said, "Here it comes …"

The woman paused. "All right, let's make it ten dollars a month."

"Score!" Jim said, slapping Nathan on the back. "Talk about a widow's mite! That was a nice upsale. After mandatory expenses, this couple has just under 62 dollars per month for books, newspapers, yarn, birthday cards, and other things to make their lives more pleasant, *and* for donations to your ministry. Now they have ten dollars less, every month. And they did it in response to an offer of North Carolina pine sap, packaged in China, that cost you a dollar including shipping. You're in the black on your first month. Nice!"

Nathan looked around at the old man staring dully at the television, at the woman putting down the telephone handset, and at their shabby apartment. He imagined how much of his own monthly incidentals 62 dollars would cover.

Jim said, "That line is a winner—'The bigger the need, the bigger the seed.' And do you know what her need is? She wants her husband to get better. Physically, he's strong, but his dementia has progressed so that he's little more than conscious. Or, failing that, she wants a release—let his physical health decline along with his mental health. Can you deliver that?"

"But that's God's job," Nathan said.

"You promised the hundredfold return. You've convinced her that you can deliver a miracle. Don't take payment for what you can't deliver."

"Look, this isn't what I wanted."

"This is exactly what you wanted. This woman has a big need—she wants what medicine says is impossible. She wants what even a billionaire can't buy. So what should she do? God can't multiply what you don't sow, so sow that big seed. Dig deep. Make it hurt. And who better to spend that ten dollars a month than you, right? You scratch their itch, so you're entitled to take a little something for your trouble. You're a smart guy and probably a better steward of her money than she is."

Nathan felt like he was up to his waist in quicksand. "But that isn't what I meant."

Jim leaned down slowly and put his huge face in front of Nathan's. It was like facing an annoyed bull. "Next time you put gas in your 600-horsepower Mercedes," Jim said, "remember who's paying the bill."

☙

Jim put his hand on Nathan's shoulder. "Take a look at someone else who watches your show."

The scene dissolved into another small apartment. One wall was bare red brick and the other walls and ceiling were painted a stark white. The precise edges brought to mind pieces of machinery. The artwork was spare—some modern art, a Broadway poster, and a poster of the movie *Brokeback Mountain*. The floor was blonde wood. An angular tan couch and frosted glass coffee table sat on a coarse sisal rug, and a thin silver artificial tree hung with small red balls stood in a corner.

The wall in front of the couch had a window and a wide-screen television. Through the window, Nathan could see a row of brownstones, and on the television he again saw his own Christmas Day broadcast.

A man with a trim goatee sat on the couch. He looked about forty-five.

Another man walked up and stood behind him. "Ben, why are you watching *him?*"

"Guilty pleasure, I guess."

"I see the guilty part. The guy hates fags."

"Not fags—faggotry. He's a 'hate the sin, love the sinner' guy."

The standing man walked around the couch and sat.

Jim nudged Nathan. "You've got an ally. And I see why the gays watch you. You're cute for an old guy!" He laughed and smacked Nathan on the butt. Nathan hadn't been in a situation that he hadn't physically dominated in a long time.

"Anyway, it's Christmas," said Ben, "time to get a dose of Christianity."

"Don't you know when you're not wanted? Homosexuality is an abomination. In their eyes, *we* are an abomination."

"Some churches have come around."

"How? The Bible must be unambiguous on the issue."

Ben said, "Lots of things were abominations in the Old Testament—ham sandwiches, lobster bisque, wearing a wool-blend suit—but those were ritual abominations. They were always separate from the things that actually caused harm like lying or murder. The sacrifice of Jesus freed people from ritual abominations. The Bible says nothing about loving monogamous gay relationships."

"Not everyone got the memo. How do they explain God making people gay and then demanding that they deny who they are?"

"The Bible gets some things right. 'Love is patient, love is kind. It does not envy, it keeps no record of wrongs.' And there is progress. Who could've imagined that we'd live to see gay marriage such a popular topic?"

"So we just wait till the old guard dies out? They whine about promiscuous gays, but when a couple wants to commit to monogamy, they reject them."

Ben laughed. "They also whine about the decline of marriage, but what do they do when the gay community wants to support marriage? If they don't like gay marriage, they can avoid getting gay married."

The second man patted Ben on the thigh. "I prefer ice cream as a guilty pleasure, but if this works for you, merry Christmas." He got up and left as the Hundredfold Singers on the television did another set.

Jim said, "So where did the anti-gay come from?"

"It was central to Lloyd's position when I came on board."

"Then drop it. You're the boss now."

"My demographic is conservative. They demand a hard anti-gay stand."

"Tough guy like you afraid to say what needs to be said? That surprises me. It sounds like a leadership opportunity—just tell them what they need to know."

"That'd be suicide. In my industry, you tell them what they want to hear. They want reinforcement of their beliefs. New ideas aren't good for business. If I pushed for reform, I'd only make myself irrelevant."

The giant turned to face Nathan. "Damn—doesn't integrity mean anything? How can you live with yourself?"

But it was just a pitch. Sure, he was a relentless salesman, but he didn't put a gun to anyone's head. People gave willingly, and that brought them a sense of peace, a sense of being part of a greater, glorious whole.

It had become sport for him, with donations as the score. He always wanted to improve his high score, but the stakes were bigger than he'd admitted. In his mind, no one got hurt, but in the real world, perhaps it was a different matter. Nathan looked at the man on the couch and thought of his college friend Gary who had bought into Nathan's Christian anti-gay message and tried to kill himself. Heck—maybe this guy had confronted the same feelings.

Jim said, "With all the problems in the world—disease, poverty, famine, natural disasters, war, jobs—*this* is near the top of your list of things that keep you up at night? You can't find something else to worry about? If you don't like gay people, then tell straight people to stop having gay babies."

CS

The apartment faded and now they were in a darkish auditorium with a couple of hundred people in the audience. A projected image behind the stage read, "Annual Christian Apologetics Conference" with the logo of the hosting college. Nathan had heard of the conference but had never attended.

The speaker was in the middle of a rant cautioning his audience to avoid Christian leaders who gave poor teachings. He enumerated many well-known preachers and other defenders of Christianity and called them opportunists, celebrities, and salesmen. In the category of televangelists, he said, "The one exception is Nathan Thorpe."

Jim patted Nathan on the back, though Nathan wondered if a dark cloud would soon envelop this silver lining.

"Beware empty rationalizations," the speaker said. "You must be harder on your own arguments than the nonbeliever you're trying to convert. Never start with a presupposition, like 'The Bible is accurate history' or even 'God exists,' and then find a way to select facts to support that. Rather, consider *all* the facts and see where they lead you. And that's where Rev. Thorpe is a good example."

Nathan had a weekly segment during which he responded to viewers' questions, which must have been what the speaker was referring to. Nathan avoided the Dear Abby category—issues like, "My boyfriend is cheating on me." He preferred questions that wrestled with intellectual arguments for and against Christianity like those in his Tough Questions folder. Like the scab that you can't leave alone, the questions remained for Nathan open and raw. He probably thought about them too much, but they were unavoidable. They were to him the boulder that Sisyphus was condemned to roll up the same hill every day.

"Let me commend Rev. Thorpe's method to you," the speaker said. "He's very well read on the subject and yet he's honest and open. If he doesn't know, he says so. But behind that gentle humility is a rock-solid faith."

Jim patted him again, though congratulatory pats from Jim's enormous palm now felt like a beating. "See there? You have a rock-solid faith. I bet that's important for someone in your line of work."

But Nathan knew that this was wrong. It would be a blissful release to let go and let God, to just take that leap of faith, certain that God would catch him. So many others had, but for him that path wasn't an option.

The speaker went on about Nathan's apologetics—his arguments were "brilliant," "devastating," "insightful," and so on. Each compliment was a lash, a reminder that his on-screen confidence was fake.

Nathan could rationalize away intellectual attacks to shore up his theological position, but doubts always remained. Faith wasn't a tool in areas like chemistry or engineering. Why should it be here, with the most important questions of all? Faith was no more useful than crossing one's fingers for luck.

He felt like an unethical used car salesman—he knew which cars needed new rings or shocks or brakes, but he wasn't about to advertise that. It was a nice living, but, like the cars, his arguments were not what people thought they were.

"This guy is quite a fan," Jim said. "Sounds like you've nailed it."

"Well, not as much as I'd like. And now that you mention it, maybe I could ask you about some of these issues. Like why God is so hidden or why prayer doesn't work as promised or why there is so much evil in the world."

"Try approaching things from the perspective of people, not God. Morality simply says that we should try to help people and avoid hurting them. Injecting God doesn't help."

"The Bible tells us God's perspective."

"Does it? Or does it give us people's interpretation of God's perspective? It's people all the way back to the original manuscripts. Why trust the Bible as a supernaturally inspired book?"

"But what if it's correct?"

"Surely the all-knowing creator of the universe has no complaint with your using his gift of the human mind to its fullest. Indeed, he'd have to be annoyed if you did otherwise. What would he say when things don't add up but you ignore your doubts and operate on faith? What's the point of that big brain if you ignore what it says?"

☙

Jim turned him around again. "Let's see the international impact of your ministry." They now stood outside a small one-story faded blue building. The sun hung bare and hot in a faded blue sky. Nathan could see heat waves coming off the metal roof.

In front of the building was a small cleared area of packed dirt. Beyond that, shacks and tents of every homemade type stretched as far as Nathan could see. Plastic tarps and corrugated metal covered many, but others used sacks or plastic bags as well. He could see no roads-and-avenues order to the layout, as if latecomers had squeezed in wherever they could.

A line of women, some carrying infants, stood to one side behind a coil of barbed wire. The place smelled like it had lots of latrines and too few showers.

Jim pointed at the building behind them. "This is made of cinderblock because it holds the food. Food distribution won't begin for over an hour, but sometimes they run out."

That explained the line of people. Nathan said, "Where are we?"

"A refugee camp in Kenya. The name means 'Nowhere' in Swahili. This is one of the camp's Dinka neighborhoods. The Dinka people are refugees from the civil war in Sudan.

They're predominantly Christian, and your ministry has come here to help them."

Jim turned and walked, and Nathan followed. "There are more than a hundred thousand refugees here," Jim said. "Some were driven here by war, some by drought."

They were soon on a narrow but busy road that wound among the tents. The Dinka people were tall, thin, and black. Many carried repurposed grain sacks printed with the country of origin or a relief organization. Nathan saw two men on crutches and then a teenage boy with no legs below the knee. "Land mine," Jim said.

They stopped in front of a mud brick building with a corrugated roof. "Here we are," Jim said. "Corruption can be a problem with international aid, but Sudan Christian Relief does what it claims to."

Hundredfold admittedly gave too little to good works organizations, but Nathan felt some pride that they were participating in the relief work.

They walked in, and Jim pointed to a book.

"What's this?" Nathan said.

"The New Testament in Dinka."

"Is that it?"

"Isn't that enough? You've paid for thousands of them to be printed and shipped here along with missionaries to spread the gospel. What could be more important than the word of God?"

"I mean, don't we participate in any of the relief work? Maybe food distribution or health care?"

"Does that bother you? If so, research your recipients more closely. But why should it? You're a ministry, not a soup kitchen. Spending money is an investment, and an investment must have a return—isn't that what you said?"

Nathan could find no retort.

"I want you to see another Dinka, someone who hasn't been blessed by your ministry." Nathan turned to follow Jim's gaze. The dusty jungle of the refugee camp was gone, and they were now in a rectangular dirt compound with mud brick walls. The shadows were long, but here, too, the air was still and hot. A dozen goats wandered around, and a woman in a black burqa milked one of them. Nathan walked closer. Enough of her face was showing to see decorative V-shaped scars on her forehead.

"A Dinka slave," Jim said. "This is northern Sudan, the Arab part. She was taken in a raid ten years ago, and her master bought her, a boy, and a girl. They're from the same village in the south, but they were beaten if they ever spoke Dinka. This woman and her husband were taken together, and after the month-long trip here, he was killed. He was useful as a pack animal to carry booty, but men aren't compliant enough to make good slaves. The boy was killed last year for the same reason. This woman is crippled and scarred from the beatings she's had. She's been raped so many times that she's now sterile. Her master has cows that are more valuable than her."

"How widespread is this?"

"There are twenty million slaves in the world today, in round numbers. Slavery was traditional within this tribe for centuries and only recently suppressed. It broke out again during the recent civil war."

Nathan felt sweaty just looking at the woman in the burqa. "What does the Koran say about slavery?"

"Though the Koran would argue that this master is too harsh, it does support slavery. But then, so does the Bible."

"Oh, no. Don't go there. Slavery in the Old Testament was nothing more than indentured servitude. It was basically a mechanism of debt relief. Terms were strictly limited to six years."

"That's true for fellow Jews only. About non-Jews, the Good Book says, 'You can bequeath slaves to your children as inherited property and can make them slaves for life.' "

Nathan again considered arguing. Could slavery be wrong for people to impose but right for God? But it seemed hopelessly relativistic to imagine "slavery is wrong" not being objectively true. He mentally moved intellectual chess pieces around but got nowhere. "What's your point? Why are you showing me this?"

"Don't point to the diary of a 3000-year-old tribe as an unchanging source of wisdom for today. You pick your way through the Bible, keeping the good parts and discarding the bad, using your own moral compass. *That's* where morality comes from, not this book."

Nathan had to think about that. God's support for slavery and genocide did make the Bible a poor fit for modern society. He turned to Jim.

Where was he? "Jim? Are we done here?" He turned around in place. Nothing. "Jim. *Jim!* Don't leave me here."

Fourth Stanza

Nathan wandered around the compound in his bare feet and bathrobe. The woman in black finished her milking and took the milk bucket inside. She limped as she walked.

She returned with a broom and swept the goat droppings from the courtyard. A boy of about seven, not quite as dark as her, came out of the house and scolded her briefly, or so his tone and body language suggested. The woman said nothing as she hobbled through her task. The unending cruelty of her life, with no realistic hope for relief, hit Nathan like a wave. This woman's future seemed to stretch out before her like a black sea. The thought of the millions of other slaves in similar situations seemed to suck all possible joy out of the world. Never had Nathan felt so empty and alone.

The sky had noticeably darkened. Nathan was eager to get away, and he went to a wooden gate in the compound and reached out his hand. It went through. He took a step as if the gate weren't there and found himself on the other side in a dusty alley, alone.

Though in this ghostly state Nathan wasn't a part of the world that he was immersed in, it had stained him nonetheless. He wondered if a slaughterhouse would be less cruel because at least there the animals suffered only briefly, while here there seemed to be little but suffering. He wanted to leave, to cleanse himself of this world, but he would never be able go back home, not completely. He couldn't dismiss what he had seen.

In the dusk, Nathan saw a man walking toward him far down the alley. The man was about his own height and no-ticeably stockier than the local people. He wore a white suit, also quite different. It might have been the lighting or the contrast with the dark buildings, but the man seemed to glow.

Another ghost! Someone who would rescue him. Nathan walked toward the stranger but once he could make out the man's features, Nathan stopped. He knew this man.

The ghost grinned as he approached. "Didn't see *this* com-ing, did you, Peanut Head?"

The ghost was Nathan himself.

"Where are you taking me?" Nathan said.

"Oh—here and there."

"You couldn't take me back home?"

The ghost laughed, closed the small distance between them, and put his hand on Nathan's shoulder.

CB

Nathan looked around. No more refugees or slaves sweat-ing in an African hell. Now he was in a sedate conference room. A long table filled the room, and the walls were paint-ed tan above dark wood cabinetry. The trees outside the wide window were bare. Wait a minute—that was the view out the Hundredfold window. And there was the ministry logo over the whiteboard at the head of the table. This was *his* board room.

He turned in place. The table was new and the room had been redecorated, but there could be no mistake.

He and the ghost were alone. A bank of four large television monitors, also new, filled most of the wall at the other end.

Nathan said, "I know this room, but it's changed. Is this the future?"

"It's your future."

He walked to the wall of monitors. Each showed a different program, but the audio for only one was on. He scanned the images—all apparently religious shows—and found the one that matched the audio.

"You're news," the ghost said as he gestured to that video. On it, two men sat in large chairs in a living room-like set. Leafy garlands with red balls spilled off a table behind them. They were in the middle of a summary of Nathan's career. Nathan didn't recognize the men or the logo of the program.

"But Brother Nathan's ministry was touched by trouble," one man said. "He paid hush money to one staffer to keep internal documents secret. Then affairs with other staffers came to light, each causing a public scandal. Three marriages, three divorces, and charges of harassment and then embezzlement as the ministry slowly lost its relevance. Unfortunately, Brother Nathan's high profile meant that he could do a lot of damage as well as a lot of good for the church."

"What is this?" Nathan said. "I'll sue—these are all lies."

"They won't be," said the ghost.

Nathan couldn't put much past the previous ghosts, but as he looked at the figure that could be his own reflection, he knew that he would be able to keep no secrets.

A door opened behind them, and two young women came in, the first with an easel and the second with Nathan's board portrait photo. Nathan didn't recognize either woman.

"Turn them off," one of them said, gesturing to the monitor, and the other pushed a wall button. The audio feed stopped.

The women arranged the portrait on the easel in the corner at the head of the room. One then set out agendas at eight places around the table, while the other shook out a long rectangle of cloth, black with purple edging. She draped it over the top edge of Nathan's portrait so that it hung down evenly on either side.

"Wait—I'm *dead?*" Nathan said.

"It happens to the best of us."

He walked over to the portrait as the women left the room. "This picture is unchanged. Do I die in the near future?"

"On, no. You've got quite a few years left. What also doesn't die quickly is your vanity. As you aged, you didn't bother updating your board photo."

"Those vultures on that show," Nathan pointed to the video they had been watching, "they just want to carve up my market share."

"It's a tough industry."

The women opened the double doors to Sophia's office, which for board meetings held the catered buffet. Judging by the warm smells, that tradition remained. Seven men and a woman walked out, only half of whom Nathan recognized, and those looked a good twenty years older than when he knew them. After a few more minutes of socializing, one man called the meeting to order and everyone found seats. The man was Frank Daubs, a local minister Nathan had known for years. He had a short gray beard over chubby cheeks. Apparently he was now the vice chair.

"Thank you everyone for coming on such short notice," Frank said, "some of us from around town and others from across the country. It's especially good of everyone to make it during the holiday season."

Nathan said to the ghost, "Some meetings it's hard to get a quorum, but it's not surprising everyone's here. It's a power play. They want to make sure their man takes over."

"It's the Borgias and Medicis fighting to elect the pope all over again," the ghost said.

Frank continued. "It's good to see everyone, though a shame that a sad occasion brings us here." He glanced at Nathan's portrait. "I'll begin by summarizing what the bylaws tell us to do in this situation. Our board serves only in an advisory capacity. Nathan, as president, had no obligation to accept our advice. But now, without a president or designated successor, we go from having no power to having all of it. We must select someone new, and we must do it quickly. The programming staff is rerunning old content. Donations are up at the moment as a sympathy response, but that won't last long. For the health of the ministry, we need a new personality in place quickly.

"Nathan was a giant in the industry, but it must be said that this ministry has been sliding for years. Nathan's age was one factor, and we all know the damage caused by the scandals. Nathan was a man of strong drives, both for good and bad.

"We now have the responsibility and privilege of replacing one of America's greatest televangelists."

Nathan grimaced. It wasn't that the label was hollow praise. In the half of his career that he knew about, he had already cast a long shadow over his field. Instead, he was beginning to wonder if that was actually a compliment.

One thin man, a stranger to Nathan, cleared his throat and said, "I raise this only as due diligence. We probably should consider all options. I'll just come out and say it: should we dissolve the ministry? The assets could be donated to worthy organizations."

Silence. Nathan scanned the faces. A few glanced up as if savoring a profound bit of wisdom. Others looked as if the man had loudly farted.

"I appreciate your bringing that up." This was Thomas Garcia, a fellow televangelist who targeted the Hispanic market. Nathan never much liked him. He had dealt with Thomas using the axiom, "Keep your friends close and your enemies closer." Still, Nathan was surprised he was still around.

"That is worth considering," Thomas said, "but we can't underestimate the powerful impact this ministry has and the lives it transforms. A world without Hundredfold Ministries would be a darker world." Several heads nodded in approval. "But let me throw out another option. Would the impact be greater still if Hundredfold could be replanted? We have our own ministries that could absorb different assets—the building, the equipment, the spectrum, the brand, the product titles, maybe the staff. That might also let us step away from any residual problems with the scandals." More nodding of heads.

"This is bullshit!" Nathan said. "He wants to hand out pieces of my ministry as Christmas presents? I worked on building this for decades, and he treats it like a buffet."

His fists clenched as others delicately supported the idea. A plan for who got what took shape. Within ten minutes, any polite pretense of hesitancy was gone and the motion of distribution was made and passed.

Nathan felt like a roast pig attacked by hungry Visigoths.

ᬠ

The ghost gestured behind Nathan. As he turned, the scene changed to a darkened lecture hall. No—a church. The ceiling was slightly arched like the building had originally been a bowling alley or large bookstore.

From the stage, the pastor said, "Today is the last Sunday of the month, the service at which we particularly welcome newcomers. Apologies to those who've heard this before, but I'll give a brief introduction to New Harvest church. We are part of the Christian Revival Movement. For decades, Christianity has had a growing problem with disbelief among its members. In an increasingly technological society, belief in a god from a 3000-year-old Iron Age culture can be hard to maintain. In some churches, twenty percent of members might've been without faith, but those members would've been embarrassed to admit it.

"But is that a problem? Redefine it as an asset—these are people eager to participate in our community and contribute time and money to our good works. Jesus said, 'Whatever you did for the least of my brothers and sisters, you did for Me.' Good-hearted atheists believe in helping the less fortunate just like the best Christians. How is this not a good thing? We're a Christian church that embraces believers, questioners, agnostics, and atheists as members. That makes for more interesting theological discussions, let me tell you.

"Belief is simply not an option for everyone—try believing in invisible pink unicorns and see how far you get. Here, faith is no longer a requirement, no longer an *obstacle*.

"We see this as an authentic interpretation of Christianity. The parable of the sheep and the goats shows the Son of Man separating people by how they cared for their fellow man, not by what they believed."

The preacher signaled to the pianist, who played the opening stanza of a hymn. As the congregation stood and sang, it sounded surprisingly traditional—maybe Bach?

The ghost said, "This is a new development—cultural Christianity. Faith is optional."

"But then it's not Christianity," Nathan said.

"That's what they always say, but that hasn't stopped new spinoffs."

"How can it be authentic? The Bible is unchanging."

"And the interpretation is not. Christian Science, Mormonism, Pentecostalism, Seventh-Day Adventists, Jehovah's Witnesses—America is fertile soil, and Christianity is nothing if not adaptable." The ghost pointed to the preacher. "This is one way Christianity will continue to evolve."

The congregation finished the hymn and sat. Once everyone had quieted, the preacher said, "Perhaps you've heard that Nathan Thorpe has died. 'America's greatest televangelist,' some have called him." He paused and smiled. "It's hard to imagine so different an approach to Christianity from our own. I hope you'll excuse my frankness, but Reverend Thorpe's line was, 'Give me lots of money so I can preach to more people that I can guilt into giving me yet more money.' We have a very different approach. We say, 'Give us time and money and let's work together to help other people, like Jesus did.' Reverend Thorpe said that Jesus commanded each of you to spread the gospel message—'Go and make disciples of all nations.' But the gospel of Matthew makes clear that this Great Commission was a charge to the disciples, not to ordinary people like us. We preach, all of us, but we believe in preaching the gospel with lives honorably lived."

The ghost said, "This is a new interpretation of Christianity. What do you think?"

℃

Nathan didn't know what to think. The tough questions that had plagued him—why God lets bad things happen to good people, why God insists on staying hidden, and so on—would be redefined into irrelevance with this new view. It was like Alexander untying the Gordian Knot with a slice of his sword.

Nathan turned in response to the ghost's gaze. They were now at a cemetery. The sun was low on the horizon, and the few leafless trees bent in the wind. About twenty paces away, a cluster of several dozen warmly dressed mourners surrounded a gravesite.

Nathan searched for familiar faces. Frank Daubs from the board was conducting the service, and Nathan picked out most of the other board members. He saw much sniffling and eye-dabbing, which seemed more theatrical than heartfelt. Sophia was there. He wondered if she had been his secretary until the end.

He was grateful that the ghost placed the two of them away from the grave. If Nathan Future were the center of attention over there, he'd rather be over here.

"I don't see Janice," Nathan said.

"She's not here. Your third ex-wife is, though." The ghost pointed to a fifty-something stranger with blonde hair covered with a black scarf. "But we're not here to see her." He gestured to Nathan's left.

Nathan jumped as he saw his sister Luna just inches away, oblivious to him. She was much older than he was now—

probably in her seventies. His kid sister now looked like their mother. It was strange to see her as his senior, in the position of authority.

Next to Luna was a woman a generation younger. That must be Margaret. She supported her mother by the arm.

"Why isn't Luna with the rest?" Nathan said. "If anyone has the right to be here, she does."

"Look who's present," the ghost said. "It's mostly the inner circle from your ministry. No one excluded her, but she doesn't feel comfortable with this group."

The service concluded, and the circle of people at the gravesite slowly dissolved. A few decided that saying something to Luna was appropriate, and the others in the group silently followed that example.

Luna took a step backwards as she saw the crowd filing her way, but Margaret held her ground and patted her mother's hand. The confused look on Luna's face vanished, and she straightened her posture to accept the condolences of the black-clad mourners. Some were silent, giving just a handshake and a smile, and others introduced themselves. Many offered "God bless you" or "He's in a better place." A woman with a black boa held a handkerchief to her face as she said, "He was a great man."

The last person in line was Sophia, and it seemed as if time had not been her friend. Though younger than Luna, she didn't look it now. She asked Luna what she could do to help, and Luna thanked her but said that she was fine. It was the expected interchange for the situation, but Sophia, devoted to the end, seemed genuinely concerned and willing to help.

Finally alone, Luna walked to the gravesite, supported by Margaret.

"If I hear one more 'God bless,' I won't be responsible for my actions," Luna said.

"Mom, it's just what people say," Margaret said, "like 'bless you' when you sneeze."

"And that 'great man' comment—Nathan hadn't been a great man for a long time, and I blame that ministry. The power was corrupting."

"If he changed into an unpleasant person, you could've just left him alone, just ignored him."

"And I did, but it was such a loss. He would've been a great courtroom lawyer or physicist or just about anything. He was a terrific TV charlatan because he was terrific at everything he set his mind to. Imagine what his intelligence could have done if applied to a noble project. The Nathan I grew up with would've made a great uncle."

"I always thought Uncle Nathan was very generous," Margaret said. "He sent great presents."

Luna was silent.

Nathan said, "Sophia did that. She kept track of birthdays and graduations and arranged for the appropriate gifts and cards." He looked at Margaret. "This is my family, but I've ignored them. My niece has grown up, and I delegated my role as uncle as if it were a chore." He wanted to say something to them, to apologize, to erase the past.

Margaret said, "Why was he so distant?"

"It was my fault," Luna said. "I wouldn't compromise, I wouldn't back down. Nathan getting religion wasn't that big a deal—it was like he was a sports fan. But once he got into that ministry, things changed. The bad outweighed the good, and I told him so.

"But I took it too far. I delighted in pointing out the errors in his thinking. Finally, I could beat my brother in an argument. I was uncompromising, and I let an argument get in the way of family. Don't let that happen to you, honey."

Nathan shook his head. "No, it was my fault. My faith was fragile, so I threw everything I had into defending it. An attack on my beliefs became an attack on my ego, and I couldn't let that stand."

Luna said, "No matter how old I got, he was always four years older. No matter my accomplishments, he was always my big brother. I think that colored our relationship."

"It did," Nathan said. "I would happily play the big brother card when I was out of better options." He looked at her sad face, wrinkled with age. She wasn't his little sister now, and he spoke to her as if she could hear him. "I told myself it was about money, about how I didn't want to be hit up for this or that expense, but that was never it. I pulled away because you held my feet to the fire. Your arguments hit home, though I wouldn't admit it. It was intellectual karate for you, but from my standpoint, you were punching holes in my lifeboat."

☙

Nathan sighed. "This is enough. I don't need to see any more."

The ghost put his hand on Nathan's shoulder, and the cemetery dissolved into a trailer park. "One final visit," he said.

These trailers weren't prefab homes with white picket fences but the old-fashioned kind with a hitch at one end. Cinderblocks held the rusting wheels off the ground. Weedy grass separated the trailers, packed tight so that only a parking space separated one from the next.

They stood next to the steps of one trailer. A faded awning shielded part of the parking space, making little difference on this cloudy winter day, and lines of rust dribbled down from the lower corners of the door.

"Why are we here?" Nathan said.

"We're waiting for the lady of the house," the ghost said.

An old compact car drove into the development and slowly wound its way to stop in front of them. Sophia stepped out, wearing the same black dress Nathan had seen her wearing at the funeral.

"Sophia, here? But Sophia has a house."

"She had a house. Larry's medical expenses took so much of their income that they defaulted on it. Sophia still works at Hundredfold, and Larry gets subsidized health care. Though Larry would disagree, it's Sophia and society that provide for him, not God."

The ghost gestured for Nathan to follow Sophia up the steps.

"I'm back," Sophia called out as she entered.

Nathan and his double walked up the stairs. The trailer would have been cozy for one, but it was cramped for two. It smelled like cooked meat, sweat, and garbage. It was laid out with the bedroom on one end, television room at the other, and kitchen in the middle. In addition to a few photos of Kay, the primary decorations on the walls were Christian talismans—a Catholic painting of Mary with her heart on fire, a Russian icon, several crosses and crucifixes, prayer beads, and contemporary pictures of Handsome Jesus with stylishly long hair and trim beard that might've been at home on black velvet. Larry reclined in a motorized chair in front of a blaring game show on television.

"What religious tradition is this?" Nathan pointed to the walls.

"This is 'All of the above' Christianity. Larry never met a healing claim he didn't like. There's a box full of more religious charms in the closet. They've been to every faith healing event within driving distance for the last fourteen years, and that's been expensive. If healing claims came with a money-back guarantee, they might still be in their house. You'd think that they would've realized that God doesn't care, that none of this works. But when they fail, they blame themselves and double down on Christian magic."

Larry said, "So, Mr. Moneybags got all boxed up and sent home?" He had been overweight before, but now he was grossly so. He wore a pajama top, sweatpants, and socks.

"Nathan's gone, Larry," Sophia said. "Not much use in complaining about him now."

"I don't know why you even had to go. He doesn't care—he's dead."

"Funerals are for the living."

Nathan said, "What's Larry's problem?"

The ghost said, "His attitude problem is that you didn't give Sophia money to cover his medical expenses. His physical problem is diabetes that has damaged his legs and feet. He hasn't worked in over a decade—not that he was an especially reliable breadwinner before."

"What happened to Kay?"

"She died from complications from her heart condition at age seventeen."

The previous day, Nathan hadn't seen Sophia as any more than an employee, but this news suddenly felt personal. "That had to destroy Sophia."

"The meaning she found in life pretty much disappeared, and she's tended her ungrateful husband and an unresponsive deity ever since. For Sophia, the church has been like caring for Larry, and it's been a one-way relationship in each case. She trusted each, and each has let her down."

"When's dinner?" Larry said, his eyes fixed on the television.

Sophia said nothing as she sat at the breakfast table, her back to Larry and the television. She looked ahead blankly as she sipped a cup of coffee.

"This is about as good as it gets for her," the ghost said. "She has a moment to herself away from washing Larry and fetching things for Larry and making meals for Larry and cleaning up after Larry and getting meds for Larry and helping Larry walk and wiping Larry after he uses the toilet. And now, her job is in jeopardy—her one excuse for connecting with other people."

"Doesn't she get out? Meet with friends or family?"

"Why should she have a social life when Larry doesn't? That wouldn't be fair, and Larry forbids it. Life for Sophia is going to her job, tending to Larry, and then conducting various prayer rituals with him at night. Each day is like the last. She's put all her expectations on the life in the hereafter and has given up on this one."

Nathan looked at Sophia and saw the Dinka slave—a world apart and very different in appearance, but alike just the same. Both were shackled to unforgiving masters. Both were Christian, but their faith solved no problem. At best, it dulled life's pain.

He considered her again. Now he saw his own life. He had cut a bigger swath through society, but his life had no greater meaning. His Hundredfold ministry, the focus of his career, had been taken apart and sold for scrap, though it wasn't like it had contributed to society. Lloyd was right—his life was a missed opportunity. Sophia had little to squander, but he had wasted much.

"Spirit, why show me this? All this—the past, present, and future? Is this just torment, just to show me the emptiness of my life?"

Nathan's ghostly self said nothing.

"What's the purpose?"

"The purpose in life? You tell me."

"I mean the ultimate purpose."

"Why imagine there's an ultimate purpose? You're a smart guy—if you want a purpose in life, give yourself one."

Fifth Stanza

Nathan opened his eyes. He remembered being very tired, and before that ... his memory of the visitations came flooding back. Lloyd, Wisdom, Jim the giant, and his ghostly double—he remembered them all.

And now he was back in his bedroom, in his bed. A pale light came from the sitting room. He got up, surprised to see that he had on the same bathrobe he had worn during his adventures, and walked toward the light. He was alone. Out the window was a sunny winter morning. Beautiful! The ghosts were done with him, and he was back home.

But was that true? He didn't know what to trust. His watch said 9:23 AM, December 25. Could it be unreliable? He walked back for his cellphone. The time, date, and year checked out, as did the GPS indication of his location. What could he conclude but that the ghosts had done their time-traveling work in one night and that it was now Christmas Day?

He flopped back on his bed. His mind was now expanded too far to be squeezed back into the box of convenience he'd kept it in. *Give myself a purpose?* he thought, remember what the last ghost had said. *Just watch me.*

Where to start? So much to do! He sprang from the bed, pulled a track suit from the closet, and put it on as he walked out of his bedroom.

He patted the railing as he ran downstairs—nice and solid. It felt good to be able to interact with the world again. "Janice!" Oops—no, she was visiting relatives.

In his office he brought up on his laptop information about the handful of nonprofits that the ministry controlled. He scanned a summary and found one that had what he needed. It could donate to both domestic and international charities.

He called the Hundredfold lawyer at home. "Frank? It's Nathan."

"Nathan! Merry Christmas."

"And a merry Christmas to you. Sorry to bother you on Christmas Day, but I have a quick question. I see Hundredfold Helping Hands as one of our nonprofits. I want to put in more money, but I need to check on governance."

"That has a board of one—just you. But you can expand that if you want."

"No, one is fine for now."

"Just keep in mind that this is a one-way street. I know it's the season of giving, but any transfer is irrevocable and can't be transferred back out to Hundredfold."

"I wouldn't want it any other way. Thanks, Frank."

In an unmarked folder in the back of a file drawer, Nathan pulled out the access information for the asset management account. Though he often approved financial matters, he so rarely made a transfer himself that he hadn't memorized the protocol. A fingerprint was required at one point and passwords at two more. After a quick transfer of assets, he logged off.

Onto the next item. He looked at his calendar for the previous day and brought up the appointment with James Truman from Ethical Christianity. Sophia was usually quite thorough in the information she recorded about Nathan's appointments and, sure enough, there was Truman's complete contact information. He picked up the phone. It might be crossing the line to call on Christmas day, but this was important.

"Hello?"

"Mr. Truman? This is Nathan Thorpe."

"Oh—hello, Reverend Thorpe."

"Mr. Truman, I know it's Christmas, so I'll make this brief. First, I want to apologize for the reception I gave you yesterday. In thinking about it further, I must admit that you make a convincing case. I'm sorry I didn't realize it sooner."

"Well, thank you, Reverend."

"Call me Nathan. I have a Christmas present for you. I am now ..."—he paused to make sure he put the correct spreadsheet into a blank email—"sending you a spreadsheet summarizing our ministry's revenue and expenses for this year, and the salaries and other compensation for the board and me." He added Truman's email address and sent it.

"This is ... unexpected."

"And perhaps a little unbelievable? Given my treatment of you yesterday, I wouldn't be surprised. You read what I've sent you, and we'll talk further. I want to see this kind of openness across the industry. I'll do what I can to help you make it happen, shaming others if necessary."

"What limitations do you put on my use of this information?"

"None. Make it public. We'll be doing that ourselves with an IRS 990 soon, so if you want the scoop, I suggest you move quickly. If you want a joint statement, email it to me and I can approve it."

"We can get that out today. Nathan, I can't thank you enough."

"Make good use of that information, and we both benefit. Merry Christmas, Mr. Truman."

"Merry Christmas!"

Nathan had one more email to send. To Peter Baldwin, the blackmailing merchandising manager who had so angered him yesterday, he wrote, "You were exactly right about the money. This isn't how a ministry should be run. Thanks for setting me straight.

"You're fired."

☙

Nathan checked his watch—almost 11:00 AM. He went to the office closet and found a red box in the shape of a large book. Since no stores would be open today, this would have to do as a gift. He picked up his car keys and wallet. In the back corridor, he stopped at Lloyd's photo and straightened it. "I always liked that picture of you," he said and walked out to the car.

He passed a gas station and remembered who paid for the gas in his car. It would take about ten seconds to pump in the monthly donation of the old couple that he and Jim had visited. He eased off the accelerator.

In front of Sophia's house, he found a parking space. With the red box in hand, he walked up the stairs to the front door. He'd never been here before—on the outside, at least.

He rang the doorbell, and Kay answered. "Mom, it's for you," she called out.

Sophia came to the door. "Nathan—merry Christmas!"

"Merry Christmas. I hope I'm not interrupting. Could I come in?"

"Of course." Sophia led him to the dining room table, not yet set for dinner. Warm Christmas smells surrounded him.

She said, "I don't think I've ever seen you in casual clothes."

Nathan looked down at his track suit, then put a hand to his unshaven chin. He combed his hair with his fingers. "This is a different look for me, isn't it? I guess today seemed like a good day to try a few new things."

Larry shut off the television and came out of the back room, dressed in the tight-fitting clothes that Nathan had last seen him in but looking more sober.

"I have a present for Kay," Nathan said.

Kay came out of the kitchen. She took the red box and opened the top. "Colored pencils, just what I wanted most!"

"Nathan, how did you know?" Sophia said.

"I have friends in high places." To Kay, he said, "I'm sorry it's not wrapped. I took it from under my tree this morning and unwrapped it, and only then did I look at the label. It said, 'To Kay from Santa.' I guess he knew I was coming over today."

"I don't believe in Santa Claus," Kay said. "Do you?"

"Well, no. I did until just recently, but not anymore," Nathan said.

"That's just for kids."

"Yes, he is. You're a smart girl."

Sophia said, "Kay, why don't you draw a picture for Reverend Thorpe to thank him for his present?"

"Okay." Kay ran to the stairs.

"Don't run!" Sophia shouted. To Nathan, she said, "Sorry about that. She can't stress her heart, and she always forgets." She gestured to the head of the table. "Have a seat."

Nathan and Sophia sat. Nathan pulled out the empty chair to his left. "Larry, join us. This affects you, too."

"This isn't bad news, I hope?" Sophia said.

"I don't think so. Remember the nonprofit work you wanted to do more of? You convinced me. I don't need a secretary, but I do need someone to spend our charitable money wisely. This nonprofit will be your new home, if you'll accept the job. I want you to be the executive director."

"Full time?"

"More than full time, at least initially. We've got a mountain of questions to answer. What should our focus be? Do we focus on disaster relief or job building or health or education or clean water or what? Do we try to influence policy? How should we split the outlay between domestic and international projects? And then, which organizations are doing the best work? It should be an interesting journey."

Larry tapped the table with a stubby finger. "Now, I'm still going to need Sophia to handle her work here."

She nodded. "Oh don't worry about that. I'll get it done."

Nathan said, "Larry, why don't *you* help around the house? I'm guessing you're out of work at the moment?"

"At the moment."

"Great—then you have some free time."

Sophia's eyes widened. Nathan imagined her mentally playing out a future scene with Larry taking out his loss of masculinity on her.

Larry said, "My job isn't cleaning and cooking. I read the Bible—wives submit themselves to their husbands, and all that."

Nathan turned to Larry. "Your job is to submit to your wife as she submits to you, Ephesians 5:21. Your job is to love your wife and not be harsh with her, Colossians 3:19. Your job is to be considerate of your wife and treat her with respect, 1 Peter 3:7. If that requires cleaning and cooking, so be it."

"Larry's right," Sophia said, waving her hands. "I can still do the housework."

"Larry's not right." Nathan said. "When the Bible conflicts with common sense, common sense wins. When the Bible is used to imprison someone, common sense wins."

Larry frowned, clearly not on board, but Nathan ignored him and said, "Anyway—you can pay for a lot of housecleaning with a salary of $100,000 per year."

Sophia's mouth dropped open.

"Oh, didn't I tell you?" Nathan said. "That's your starting salary. And, Sophia, we'll find a way to fund treatment for Kay's heart condition, we must. She's been through too much, and she can be made well; I'm certain of it."

"Nathan, I don't know what to say."

"Say you'll do it."

"Okay, I'll do it!"

Nathan held up his hand. "And I know what you're thinking. You're thinking that this salary is low for executive directors running foundations as big as this one. That's true, but we'll fix that as you grow into your job."

"How big is the foundation?" Sophia said.

"$170 million. I funded it this morning."

"But where did that money come from?"

"Hundredfold has been collecting money, waiting for the right purpose. I think helping the world's needy is the right purpose. Oh, and by the way, IRS rules require that at least five percent of assets must be distributed each year. That means we need to find a home for $8.5 million per year. We've got a lot to do."

"I'm sure I'm not ready."

"You'll learn. I'll make sure you're never in over your head. You're wise, like your name. We could call it the Rainy Day Fund."

"Or the Christmas Fund."

"Even better."

Larry flapped his hands and said, "It's not supposed to be this way."

Nathan said, "How's it supposed to be?"

"I don't know." Larry gaped like a fish. "Not like this." He shook his head. "My father was the master of his household, and I intend to be the master of mine."

"Larry, how about you and I pray for wisdom—would that work for you?" Nathan slid his chair closer to Larry and put his hand on Larry's shoulder.

Larry nodded.

Nathan remembered a story about how George Washington could crush a walnut with one thumb. He thought of that as he squeezed Larry's trapezius.

"Sophia, could you give us a moment alone?"

Larry's face showed a silent mixture of surprise and pain as Sophia stood and walked toward the stairs.

Nathan moved his hand to the back of Larry's neck and braced himself on the table with his other hand. With a sudden jerk he pulled Larry's head so that it smacked against his own, forehead to forehead. Larry grabbed the table with both hands. Nathan saw stars, but he was expecting it. He could only imagine what Larry felt.

"Ow, ow, ow." Larry mumbled.

"Listen to me, you son of a bitch," Nathan said quietly, his forehead still touching Larry's. "If Sophia *ever* comes to work beat up again, I'm going to track you down and find out why from you, and the police will be right behind me. You read me?" Nathan squeezed the back of Larry's neck. "You read me?"

"Yes!"

"If she has a black eye, if she's 'fallen down the stairs,' if she's stubbed her toe, if she wears a scarf even as a fashion statement, if she's broken a fingernail, if a hair is out of place, you will answer to me." Nathan felt energy flowing through him like electricity. "I will focus everything I've got on your sorry ass. You'll think you're an ant under a magnifying glass. Are we on the same page here?"

"Yes, yes."

"You're a bug. Do not get on the wrong side of me. Gravy train's over, pal. You clean up your act or it will be the mission of my life to make yours miserable."

❦

When Nathan left, Lloyd seemed dazed and subdued. That was the stick; Nathan would need to find ways to offer Lloyd a carrot.

At home, Janice still hadn't returned from Christmas with her relatives. He supposed she'd stay another night and he'd see her at work the next day.

Nathan had one more Christmas connection to make. This phone call would be difficult, but not in the manner of a conversation in which one must grudgingly confess an error. He knew what he had to say and was ready to say it. This would be more like asking a girl for a date, where she might be pleased or might laugh in your face.

He picked up the phone and dialed.

"Hello?"

"Luna, it's Nathan." Though he had seen her future self just the previous night, he hadn't spoken to her in real life for years.

"Nathan, what a surprise."

That was noncommittal. "Yeah, I haven't been communicative lately. Or ever. Hey, I was hoping we could patch things up. You know, be like a family again. That didn't come out right—you know what I mean."

Silence. Thoughts arose to fill the void. Maybe she was angry and didn't want to talk about it. Or wanted to vent her anger. Or didn't much care anymore. Each seemed plausible. What was she mulling over that took so long? "Luna?"

"Nathan—sorry about that. I was checking with Margaret. How would you like to have Christmas dinner with us?"

"In Boston?"

"No, we're in town visiting Margaret's husband's family. We're probably twenty miles from you." She suggested a local restaurant. "How about if Margaret and I meet you there in an hour?"

And so it was settled. Nathan could get his family back.

He stroked his chin—while he was ready to discard the narcissistic bodybuilder image, he couldn't reconnect with his family looking like a derelict.

Nathan arrived at the restaurant early, looking presentable. Twenty-four hours earlier, he didn't much care about Luna— or so he told himself. He didn't know when he'd thought about her last. But now, waiting for Luna and his niece, he felt as nervous as if he were waiting for a job interview.

When Luna arrived, her smile evaporated his anxiety.

"I'm sorry," Nathan said.

"I'm sorry, too," she said as she stepped forward to hug him.

Luna introduced Nathan to Margaret, now twenty-five. When had he seen her last? She must've been little.

Margaret's news was that she'd recently gotten married. Nathan had heard, and Sophia had sent an appropriate and generous gift for the wedding, but he had ignored the event. Now he realized what he'd missed.

After some catching up on jobs and interests all around, Nathan launched into the apology he'd rehearsed on the drive over. Luna cut him off after a few sentences. "Nathan, it's okay. I was part of the problem, too."

"It's not okay, but I appreciate your understanding."

She said, "This is so out of the blue."

Nathan wasn't sure how to respond. "To use a religious term, I guess I had an epiphany. I realized that I was grasping for the shadow, while the real thing was passing me by."

"I see you on TV occasionally," Luna said. "You've got the sexy preacher thing figured out."

"I'm sorry to hear that you've seen the show." Nathan smiled. "The sexy preacher is having second thoughts."

"What happened?"

"A crisis of faith, I guess, though it's not really a crisis. More like taking off dark glasses."

"So what do you believe?"

"I'm not sure."

"Did you quit your show?"

"No."

"An agnostic is running Hundredfold Ministries?"

"It looks like it."

"Since when?"

"Since today, though I have been suppressing my doubts for years."

Luna seemed unable to formulate more questions, and Margaret was watching the interaction.

"It's complicated," Nathan said. "I don't pretend that it makes sense. This morning, I woke up, realized that my faith could no longer hold back the tide of the questions I've been asking myself about Christianity. Then I transferred the $170 million that we had laying around into a foundation so that this ministry can give something back."

"You've had a busy day," Luna said.

"*How* much?" Margaret said.

"$170 million. We ran the ministry as a way to support a luxurious lifestyle—first class hotels, private jets, company cars, a mansion or two. I think my meal expenses last year were $300,000, but we only gave eight percent of revenue to charities. We preach a little gospel as well. Saving souls was supposed to be our primary purpose, but I really haven't believed that for years. And, over the decades, we collected a little extra cash."

"Just a little," Luna said. "How much of all this is public information?"

"Ministries and churches in the U.S. are exempt from disclosing their finances. We release some figures, and they're all accurate. My salary, for instance, which is modest. But my salary is irrelevant when I have carte blanche for basically every luxury I could want. That will change. We'll be disclosing everything."

"Is there anything embarrassing?"

"Definitely. That's why Congress gives us this exemption. Political allies in years past have given us perk after perk—

ministers' housing is deductible, their wages are exempt from income tax withholding, and every nonprofit is required to show its finances except churches. The idea is that nonprofits get a financial advantage, and in return they open their books to show that the charitable work was done as promised. But churches are exempt. That exemption acknowledges that we have something to hide. Why else would we of all groups—who say that God Almighty is critiquing how we spend our money—not be comfortable telling everyone?"

"What's next for the ministry?"

"I'm wondering that myself. I've got to do the show to-morrow, and I have no idea what I'm going to say."

❧

Nathan discussed his Tough Questions openly during din-ner, the first time he had ever done so without feeling like he was planning a crime. Luna and to a lesser extent Margaret had new insights on all facets of the questions. He envied their unconstrained intellects, but he would learn.

Back home, he collaborated with James Truman on his press release. Finding common ground was easy, and Truman promised to send it out that evening.

The next morning, he put on his suit with an ordinary shirt and tie. He wouldn't need the bodybuilding shtick anymore because he would stand out from his competitors just fine. He hadn't been this nervous in years. It was a good nervous, but he would be walking without a net.

At work a little early, he checked the Hundredfold web site press section to see if the Christmas Eve press release against homosexuality had gone out. It had. He composed a quick rebuttal that apologized for Christian excesses against homosexuals, summarized briefly how the Bible said nothing about loving gay couples, and concluded, "The Bible isn't the only word or even the last word on marriage."

He published the press release and emailed a copy to Sophia and then walked out to update her. She was at her desk, but as he began to speak, he remembered. "Sorry—I thought for a moment that you were my secretary. I forgot that you're the ED of the Christmas Fund that I've heard so much about. I just sent you an email that you can ignore."

Sophia was radiant. "We talked at Christmas dinner about nothing but the foundation. And last night I could hardly sleep, I was so full of ideas. Will you have time to go over this?"

"This afternoon. But push ahead. Don't let me hold you back."

"And Larry is changed. He's very positive now about the new job, and we're both hopeful about Kay."

"Let's discuss all that. And let Larry know that I'm here for him if he'd like to talk."

Sophia looked energized, like a wilted flower after good splash of water.

"Nathan, I need a moment." Peter Baldwin walked toward him, looking like a thundercloud.

"Looks like you got my email," Nathan said and turned to walk back into his office.

Peter followed him and closed the door. "You think I'm bluffing," he said quietly.

"I don't care if you're bluffing or not."

"I've got a long list of media organizations who would love to get this spreadsheet. I've got the names and email addresses all ready to go."

"Make my day."

Standing there and looking stupid, Peter seemed unable to understand how his stratagem didn't work. With so flawless a Plan A, he apparently hadn't thought to create a Plan B.

"Peter, look, I've got a busy day, and you're not really supposed to be here, so if you're done?"

"So I'm just out? After twelve years? Just like that? No severance?"

"On behalf of Hundredfold Ministries, thank you for your long years of service. And you don't get severance if you're fired."

"You can't fire me without cause."

"Blackmail isn't cause?"

Another pause. Peter's mouth was open, but no words came out.

Nathan said, "What? Do you need a hug? You're fired. Goodbye."

"Expect to be front page news," Peter said as he turned and left.

"I do indeed."

Nathan took out a notepad on which he had outlined the day's sermon and pushed some of the ideas around. The teleprompter always gave him the feeling of being wrapped in a comforting security blanket, but he would be naked today.

"Nathan, you've got to see this." Malcolm Canon, the speechwriter, walked in. "We should talk in private." He went back to the door. "But why bother? It's public knowledge." He returned.

"You look agitated."

"Have you seen this?" He pushed a sheet of paper with a news article across Nathan's desk. "CNN picked it up early this morning. MSNBC and Fox followed. Everyone will have it by the end of the day."

Nathan shook his head.

"An organization called Ethical Christianity claims to have our income statement—total revenue, a breakdown of expenses, the percentage donated to charity, everything. It doesn't make us look good."

"No, I imagine not."

"Nathan, do we have a mole passing along confidential information? Or did this guy just make it up? Should we be planning damage control? You may need to make a statement."

"I'll definitely make a statement, but don't worry about it. The numbers are legitimate, and I am the source."

"How ... *you* gave out the numbers? You've always protected them like state secrets."

"Nathan!" Now it was Nick the accountant. "Malcolm, I need to talk with Nathan now. Privately." Nick guided Malcolm toward the door.

Nathan called out, "Malcolm, all will be explained. Don't worry."

"Nathan, Nathan." Nick closed the door behind Malcolm and then trotted to Nathan's desk. "The Rainy Day fund is empty."

"Did you check the audit trail?" Nathan said.

"Not yet. I had an email notice of the transfer this morning and wanted to tell you first thing."

"When you check, you'll see it was me. I funded a nonprofit that will do some good with that money."

"All of it? You moved," his voice became softer, "the entire $170 million?"

"I wish I could've coordinated with you, but this was something I wanted to get done quickly. Think of it like an impulse purchase of a belated Christmas present."

"A $170 million impulse purchase?" he said hoarsely.

"No need to whisper. It's all out in the open now." Nathan stood to encourage Nick to the door. "Thanks for pointing this out. I promise to keep you in the loop in the future."

He guided Nick out, still spluttering. Nathan promised to make things clear, checked his watch, and walked to Janice's dressing room. He knocked.

"Come in." Janice was reading in a chair when Nathan walked in. The taping wouldn't begin for an hour.

"How was Christmas?"

"Good." She put down the book. Her expression was cool, though not as icy as it had been, and he saw in it the beauty that had captured him years earlier.

"Mine, too. I have a few changes in mind for today's show. We have a show in the can to run today, and we planned on taping another show. However, I want to postpone that taping and redo the sermon, live."

"Do you need something from me?"

"No. Your support, maybe. I'm taking things in a new direction."

She frowned and searched his face. He imagined she was looking for a cause such as drugs or psychosis.

He smiled. "I think I'm sane. In fact, I've never felt saner or more confident about a decision."

"Tell me about it."

"It'll probably be clearest if I get back to preparation and you watch it live."

"Did something happen to cause this change?"

"I took a hard look at myself and didn't like what I saw. I may be seeing now some of the things that have bothered you. But let's talk more about that later. Wish me luck." He patted her hand and left.

CB

"Christmas—a good time for new beginnings." Nathan stood at the podium. His notepad, full of cross outs, arrows, and exclamation points, covered the teleprompter on the lectern. He was live, and there was no safety net where gaffes could be edited out.

"You may have heard of our ministry's financial information coming from a group called Ethical Christianity." He looked at the camera with a calculated pause—no reason not to add a little drama. "The facts and figures that they give are accurate. I know because I was the source. What it shows is that our expenses are high, and the amount that we pass on to charities is low. In short, we have been a poor steward of the money you have given us. To begin to right that wrong, we have put $170 million into a foundation we're calling the Christmas Fund. The executive director is Sophia Becker, a long-time employee."

Nathan looked out at the production crew. The floor manager stood at the front of the stage and stared at him, his mouth slightly open and his clipboard by his side.

"Doing the right thing can be hard," Nathan said. "I've told you that myself many times from this stage. Now, it's our turn to take the difficult step. We will be filing a tax form 990, which all nonprofits are required to file publicly, with churches like ours an exception. And now you know why—sometimes churches have things to hide.

"Our information is finally public, and I encourage all ministries to follow suit. To them I say, if we're comfortable with God seeing our finances, why not our fellow citizens who foot the bill?

"Let's tear down this curtain of secrecy. You want the finances of a cult opened up? Tell Congress. You're proud that your church has nothing to hide? Tell Congress. Even if your church is one of the good ones that opens its books to the public, the cloud of suspicion hangs over every church with this exemption in place.

"Let me show you how things work here." Nathan pulled from his pocket a vial of the Balm of Gilead that had been so successful, and he explained that it was just pine sap. He gave its cost and the average income that each vial had brought in. "This was not a five percent return, like what a grocery story might get for a typical sale. This was a 6000 percent return." He went through a few of the other giveaways and ridiculed them one by one. "Everything we did was legal. Not a lot was right."

Nathan looked at the image on the monitor going out live to the world. For once, at Nathan's insistence, the Prayer Requests text was not displayed. He wanted to wait a day or so until he could make clear what they were asking for and why.

"All the preaching I gave you was accurate. The Bible does say that to those who give, God will throw open the floodgates of heaven and pour out so much blessing that there won't be room enough to store it.

"But did you wonder why I didn't say, 'Sell everything you have and give to the poor'?" Jesus said that. I didn't bring that up because it wasn't convenient for my message. The Bible is a mirror, and you see yourself in it. If you're wealthy or want to be, Jesus is eager to give you lots of money. If you're poor or are concerned for the poor, Jesus said, 'It is easier for a camel to go through the eye of a needle than for a rich man to enter the kingdom of God.'

"People ask, 'What would Jesus do?' but the problem isn't figuring out what Jesus would do. That's easy; we just don't want to do it. Jesus helped the poor and vulnerable. We've become like the rich young ruler who was eager to do the right thing until he found out that it was inconvenient. I pledge that this ministry from now on will strive to do the right thing, and we'll be transparent so that you can check."

The timer was counting down the final seconds. He needed to end at the right moment so that this live sermon would fit exactly into the slot held by the taped one. He had to hurry.

"Let me leave you with a final thought. God gave you your big brain to use. Trust based on evidence is good. Faith based on wishful thinking is not. The ultimate insult to God would be to check your brain at the door when you go into a church. Or to accept things because you'd like them to be true or because an authority told you so, not because of good evidence. If you're skeptical, if something doesn't make sense, if you have doubts, that's God's brain warning you. Listen to that advice.

"I'll see you tomorrow."

&

The red light on the camera blinked off. Nathan looked at Janice in the wings as he walked to the chair at the back of the stage. She gave him a smile and a thumbs up. He dropped into the chair, elated and exhausted.

The stage manager walked up to him. "Okay, Nathan. We're back to the recorded close." He moved the clipboard from one hand to the other. "Well, that was some show."

"What did you think?"

"I don't know what to think, but I do wonder what the plan is moving forward."

"I wonder the same thing. Hey, could you spread the word that I'd like to have a meeting with everyone, here, in say ten minutes?"

"No need to wait. They're all here. As soon as everyone heard that you were going off script, they came to listen." He motioned for the house lights to come up, and Nathan could see the crowd against the back wall.

Nathan walked to the front of the stage. There was no need to call everyone's attention because all eyes were on him. "Come in closer. We might as well get friendly."

The staff silently walked in.

"I owe you an explanation. We're moving in a new direction, but you probably already know that.

"Let me get personal for a moment. I've been struggling with my faith for years. That was inconvenient, so I did my best to suppress it, but the questions wouldn't go away. Like, why are so many prayers unanswered, even unselfish ones? Sure, we tell ourselves that God always answers and that sometimes the answer is 'No' or 'Not yet,' but then what role does God play? I could pray to a stump and get the same results.

"Why is God hidden? Since he knows how vital it is for us to believe the right things, why isn't he as obviously real as the sun?

"Why do bad things happen to good people?"

He looked out over the crowd. He had never seen himself as a teacher and never visualized the people on the other side of the camera, but here were faces that he couldn't ignore. Here were real people who had helped build his success and took what he had to say seriously, anxious to hear what he had to say.

"Have you heard the story of the Gordian Knot?" he said. "Alexander the Great came upon a famous knot so complicated that no man could untie it. He finally succeeded—with a swing of his sword.

"And that's the solution here. You can, with difficulty, shoehorn these problems into a world with God, or you can take the Alexandrian solution and ask, what if there *is* no god? Then the difficulties fall away effortlessly. //

"Why are prayers unanswered? Because there is no one to answer them. Why is God hidden? Because we only imagine that he's there. Why do bad things happen to good people? Because there is no omnipotent, all-loving god looking out for us, and bad things just happen. //

"And there are lots of other questions that I'm sure many of you have wrestled with—questions about which countless books have been written by great Christian thinkers through the centuries—but the questions answer themselves if you drop the presupposition that God is behind everything. Why did God order genocide and condone slavery? Why did God make millions of people only to drown them all in the Flood? Why does early Judaism look like just another Canaanite religion? Why does good and bad befall Christians no differently than anyone else? Why are there no novel scientific truths in the Bible? Why make a big deal about the Jesus resurrection story when we dismiss as mythology earlier resurrections of gods from other cultures? Why is Christianity alone true when it's clear that humans throughout history have invented thousands of religions?"

He had spent so much time with the problems that the list came flooding out without effort.

"Personally, I'm in sort of a limbo. This thinking is new to me, and I won't accept it without a lot of consideration. But my faith—or the pretense of one—is gone. Going forward, if the only way to get to a belief is across a bridge of faith, I just won't go there. I'll wait for the evidence.

"So that's my situation, but you don't have to follow my thinking. This isn't a theocracy, and you're welcome to view Christianity however you like. Change is happening, and you should think about your careers. Everyone is welcome to stay and there will be no faith test, but if working in a conservative Christian organization is important to you, this won't be one. Peter Baldwin, for example, has already resigned."

Malcolm came up to him. "Nathan, you're not going to believe this." He handed his phone to Nathan. On it he had the Nielsen rating for the show.

Nathan held the phone out to the audience. "A twenty-two share!" he shouted. "Nielsen gave us a twenty-two share. That's unimaginably huge—twenty-two percent of Americans with their TVs on were tuned to our show. I don't think we've ever gotten more than a one share before." He turned to Malcolm. "But why? How did everyone find out?"

"We're news," Malcolm said. "That Ethical Christianity story must've gotten people going. It's all they're talking about on social media."

"This is our opportunity," Nathan said to the crowd. "We're breaking the mold, and the nation—no, the world—is listening. Let's tell them about a church that honors the teachings of Jesus without the demand of faith.

"We've got a lot to do to capitalize on this publicity. Who can we collaborate with? Who is an ally who would have a message in sync with ours? Where can we get grants? Is public television the best funding model going forward?

"The good news is that we're news. We need to ride this wave of free publicity as far as it will take us, because it won't last long. We can use it to reach out to people who wish us well far beyond conservative Christianity. And we're not starting off with a few dreamers sketching ideas around a kitchen table. We have a huge television presence and an experienced staff."

"The bad news is that we just gave away our $170 million cushion. I'm convinced that that was the right move—doing good work is in keeping with the wishes of the people who gave Hundredfold that money, but starting a new initiative, even a Christian-ish one like this, is not. God will not provide.

"I give us a fifty-fifty chance of making it, and I'm probably optimistic. Are we going down? Maybe, but not without a fight and not without making a big statement that the world can't ignore."

☙

And they did change the world, in their own way. Sophia Becker grew into her job and guided her foundation to do substantial good in the world. Kay had her operation, which fixed her chronic health problems, and, with a little coaching from Nathan, Larry found a healthy and responsible approach to his role as husband and father.

Nathan continued to work with Jim Truman. The Christian community responded by polarizing into supporters of the new transparency and traditionalists who dug in their heels. The issue was a political football within Congress, but momentum shifted so that churches' closed books and even their nonprofit status were part of the debate.

Janice and Nathan returned to their marriage and worked together to reshape the ministry to support their shared vision of a transformed Christianity. After a period of austerity, a large grant from an atheist benefactor gave them the stability to find supporters who wanted a rational kind of Christianity that celebrated rather than dismissed reason.

It soon became known as the Christian Revival Movement.

Author's Note

If you enjoyed this journey, continue it at the blog, patheos.com/blogs/crossexamined. The blog is an energetic but civil critique of Christianity, and I'd love to see you become a regular reader and participate in the discussion.

You may also enjoy my previous novel, *Cross Examined: An Unconventional Spiritual Journey*. Inspired by true events, its goal is to give thoughtful Christians something to think about—those Christians who enjoy the intellectual challenge of C.S. Lewis, for example. There are plenty of apologetic ideas to engage atheists as well.

I hope to see it succeed where nonfiction apologetics books often do not, by encouraging Christians to consider and even critique the foundations of their religion. It's an intellectual workout—a taxing project, perhaps, but one that leaves the reader a stronger person.

I've received some great advice and encouragement during this project, and I'd like to thank my critique group friends: Dave Gardner, Roger Curtis, and ...

Others read the final manuscript and provided invaluable input: Jason Black ...

I thank you all.

Proof

Made in the USA
Charleston, SC
13 August 2013